WIFE 2

Assa Ray Baker

Raneissa Baker

GOOD 2 GO PUBLISHING

Wife 2
Written by Assa Ray Baker & Raneissa Baker
Cover Design: Davida Baldwin, Odd Ball Designs
Typesetter: Mychea
ISBN: 978-1-947340-62-6
Copyright © 2020 Good2Go Publishing
Published 2020 by Good2Go Publishing
7311 W. Glass Lane • Laveen, AZ 85339
www.good2gopublishing.com
https://twitter.com/good2gobooks
G2G@good2gopublishing.com
www.facebook.com/good2gopublishing
www.instagram.com/good2gopublishing

Chapter 1

Something One Believes

AFTER EVERYTHING WENT DOWN with Peachee and Rick and I got custody of my daughter, Pooh, things settled down and I was back in the house with Donna again. It was now spring break, and the kids were about to be out of school for the summer. I was hard at work trying to bounce back from a few heavy losses I had taken over the winter. First, I got ganked by some off-brand nigga in Chi-town for ten G's on a test run to see what he was working with. If his product would have been any good, then I would've spent more with him, but it wasn't. I know in all of those movies the guys always have time to test the product before buying it. Well in real life that's not always true because exchanges are made in malls, parking lots of restaurants, and places like that, especially dealing with outta towners. So, yeah, the nigga got one off, but it was his loss for not putting his best up front first because he could've gotten us for more cash later. The worst hit was when almost simultaneously two of the spots were hit. One, three masked men ran in and robbed my guys of a few pounds of kush and a quarter thang of hard. I believe the niggas working just took the money for themselves for their trouble, but I wasn't there, so I had to take their word for it. The other, the police raided a safe house right after we got fresh. That was three and a half books down the drain.

I had to use most of the money from my car sales to put us back on. Yeah, I had cash put away in different spots. I took a $35,000 loss when Angel packed up and moved out of state because I wouldn't leave Donna and the kids for her. Which was crazy because Donna had gotten really cold with me after I dropped the divorce. I thought it was just stress from having my daughter in the house full time. Yeah, she got to see how it felt to be me with her kids as their stepparent. All her bullshit did was push me closer to Mica and kept me out in the streets more.

Really, tell me who wants to be around a sad

mutha-fucka all the time? I tried with her. I took her out, bought her all type of things. I even tried to put a smile on her face by placing dozens of different-color roses all around our bedroom along with teddy bears and the candy I knew she liked. But nothing worked. It seemed like the only time she was happy was when she was out with her sister Neek. I finally just let her be and got back focused on getting the money I needed to get up out of the streets. Not only was I tired of that life, but my family was tired of me being out there as well. My uncles made it out of the game and wanted the same for me. That's real freedom.

I was on my way back to Milwaukee from a small town upstate where I hustled the long way for weeks at a time. Hey, they paid good money not to have to drive down to the city for their party

needs, and I love driving, so it worked out fine. Anyway, I was about halfway home when I received a call from my daughter.

"Daddy, when you coming home? Because Toni keep messing with me."

Toni is Donn's youngest son. I think he was always being mean to Pooh because he had a crush on her and couldn't have her. "Baby, I'm not there yet, so you. . ."

3

"Fuck you, funky-ass bitch!"

"Put his ass on the phone now!" I couldn't believe he would be so bold knowing she was on the phone with me.

"Here, Daddy want you."

"Bitch, that's your daddy, not mines. Fuck y'all!"

His lil ass went hard. I was pissed.

"Daddy, he won't take the phone, and he said. . ."

"I heard him. Go tell Donna what's going on and tell her to keep his ass in the house until I get there."

When she went and tried to tell Donna everything, Donna snapped on her and then the line went dead. I tried to call them both on their phones but all I kept getting was voicemail. Now I was speeding to get home. I couldn't believe my baby was being treated like that. I wondered if it was that way all the time for her while I was gone and she just wasn't telling me for fear of having to go back to her mother. I planned to get to the bottom of all of it ASAP. Once I made it to the house, Donna was all dressed up ready to go out somewhere, and from the way she was dressed, it wasn't out with her damn sister either.

"Why you ain't answering my calls?"

"Boy, you know my ringer don't work, and it was

on the bed."

"I see it's in your hand now, but fuck that. How come you yelled at Pooh when I told her to call you about Toni? I was on the phone the whole time," I said, letting her know I heard it all myself.

"Boy, miss me with that shit. That bitch is yours, so you deal with her. I ain't tryin' to take care of no other bitch's kid. I got my own."

It took everything in me not to slap the living shit outta her. "Wow! So that's how you feel?" I turned to my baby, who was standing at the top of the stairs with Autumn. "Pooh, get your stuff right now!" I got up in Donna's face. "What the fuck do you think I've been doing around this bitch for all these years, but now it's an issue when you gotta do it for me?" I took a step back because I was too upset to be that close to her disrespectful ass. "Bitch, you don't gotta worry about it no mo'," I promised and then went and helped my baby get her things in the car. I told Donna I'd be back to get the few things I had there.

I called Dream on the way to her house and asked her if it was okay for Pooh to stay over there with her until I was done doing what I had to do for us. Dream said yes.

"Assa, she can stay as long as you need me to keep her here for you."

Dream had an extra bedroom since her oldest was away at school. Her other daughter was happy to have someone her age to hang out with because she was lonely without her big sister. Pooh and her got along like sisters. Me and Dream made a good team. It could've been a great one if I could have gotten her girlfriend to see that we didn't want to be with each other. I respected their relationship. Who Dream was fooling around with had nothing to do with me. As long as it didn't get in the way of our friendship, I was fine with it. Dream didn't charge me for allowing Pooh to be there, but I still gave her whatever she needed to help her out with food and bills.

Like I said, I respected her relationship. Even though my baby was there, I never dropped by without calling first because I knew how her girlfriend felt about me. I did what I could to try to put her mind at ease about us. I asked them out on a double date so she could see me with another woman. I took this thick-ass girl I met when I stopped to help her and her friends change their car tire. Anyway, I thought the night went great, but a few hours afterward, Dream called me upset and told me they had broken up. I was floored. Oh, I forgot to mention that my date was bisexual. So I guess it's true what they say about them being able to spot their kind a mile away.

Moving right along, I still had to play nice with Donna because when I took my daughter and walked out on her ass again, I wasn't thinking of myself. I had left a nice amount of weed and cash behind along with a few other miscellaneous things I wanted. So for about a week I called her and asked if I could come get my things. She told me she wasn't home and wanted to be there when I got them. Okay, I could do that. But she never called me to come meet her. I got busy, so I didn't sweat it. About a week after that she called me and asked me to come to the house and talk to her. I agreed. I really just wanted my stuff. And after I retrieved my things I was gonna let her know that she was on her own. I was done paying her way and taking care of other niggas' kids. I mean fair is fair, right?

Chapter 2

Donna

THE HEART WANTS WHAT the heart wants, and mine had been screaming for my husband. Lord knew I honestly hated myself for the way I treated his daughter. I was high as a kite that day and on some real I-don't-give-a-fuck shit. Honestly, it was much easier to accept Ray's daughter as my own when I thought we shared a child of our own. I don't know, it's hard to come up with an explanation for my behavior. After finding out the truth about Autumn, Ray didn't treat her any differently. Like I said, I messed up. Letting him cool off for awhile was the best thing for me to do because when I called, he answered and agreed to come over to talk about it after things slowed down for him.

WIFE 2

Right now, I was in my truck chauffeuring Deidra around the city. I knew if the few customers she had had us running around like that, that it was gonna be awhile before I saw Ray. I'd been with him long enough to know his people had him running nonstop. I bet you he hadn't eaten since this morning when I saw him at McDonald's drive-thru as I passed on my way to my daughter's apartment.

Maybe I'll cook him something when he come over tonight, she thought.

"I know you think you gotta handle things with that sucka-ass nigga so he don't leave you hanging, but fuck him. Real talk, ma. Just hit me with that work he left with you and let me get this money for us," Deidra said once we were back at her place.

"I don't know. I know he ain't gonna play about his money and I don't wanna push him over the edge. I don't wanna be the cause of him to stop dealing with the kids. They look forward to spending time with him."

"Ma, you gotta trust me. I got you. An' I got goons that'll handle that nigga if he try and get outta line. Believe me, Donna, I know how to make a nigga respect my gangsta."

I watched her place her gun on the table on the

9

way to her bedroom. She a goon, but I didn't think she really wanted to get into it with Ray.

"The only way I'll do something like that is if you help me move outta that house, because I don't wanna be no place where he can find me if things go bad," I told her but I was thinking about giving him his stuff back tonight and leaving her alone.

"Okay, that's not a problem," she murmured, pulling me close to her and kissing on my neck. I don't wanna be in a crib you shared with yo ex anyways," she admitted, sucking and nibbling. Her mouth felt so good on my skin.

"Don't start nothing you can't finish. You know you got people waiting on you," I told her, letting her know she was turning me on.

"I can always handle mine, and I don't start nothing I can't finish. Home comes first, right? Now shut the fuck up and trust me," she told me before kissing me hard on the lips.

I told her that I did trust her as she undressed me. I allowed myself to get caught up in the moment and helped her get my clothes off. The anticipation of what was about to go down had me of fire. Deidra pushed me down on her queen-size bed, breaking our kiss, and then slid her warm hands slowly up between my thighs. She gently stroked my silky folds, first with her fingers, then with her mouth. Her lips on my warm, wet lips. Deidra sucked on me until I couldn't stop myself from giving her what she wanted. She worked her way up my trembling body til her mouth was on my breast, neck, chin. Now I could taste my cum as she kissed me, and could feel her wetness dripping as we humped and grinded our way to breath-taking orgasms. I knew she was far from done with me when she pulled out her big black dildo. The way she was fucking me had a bitch agreeing to all the shit she was talking. We came hard together again and then drifted off to sleep locked in each other's arms.

Hours later, I was wakened by the sound of Ray's ringtone. I got up and checked the time after sending the call to voicemail. It was almost three in the fucking morning.

"Oh shit! Deidra, I gotta go. I'll call you in the morning so you can come get that stuff outta my house." I promised her, then quickly washed up and raced home.

Before I parked behind the house I circled the block to see if Ray had parked in front, because the other spot in back of the house was empty, and I knew he wasn't gone and that he was worried about me. And just like I thought, his Monte Carlo was parked right in front. I parked in back of the house in my spot. As much as I wanted to see him, I knew this wasn't going to be a good time.

"Why the fuck wasn't you answering your phone?" he demanded, meeting me at the door. "I thought something had happen to you."

"Look, I don't got time for this shit, it's late." I pushed past him and continued walking inside the house. "You're not here. You left me, remember? So why should I be here?"

"What? Because you got kids here and they need you to get your shit together. I don't give a fuck who you fucking with, but if they can't respect that you got kids and you don't feel him enough to bring him here, then you need to move on," he told me, locking the door and following me over to the couch.

"Ray, I love you. I know I was wrong. It's just so hard knowing that I messed up our family. I'm sorry, and I'm begging you to forgive me and give us another chance. I'll do better with Pooh. I don't want her hating me because I was feeling some kinda way that day." I was just saying the first thing that popped into my head trying to change his mood from being upset that I made him worry about me.

"Donna, you sound crazy as hell right now after pulling this shit here. Bitch, you had one chance to fuck over my baby! Never again. It won't happen ever again. We're done." He turned to leave,

and I just couldn't let him walk out on me again. "Donna, move. I'm not finna fight with you. Now, move!"

"No, you're not leaving until we're done talking! So move me. If you bad, muthafucka, move me!" I snapped.

"Girl, gon with that petty shit!"

When he tried to go around me, I went wild swinging and hitting him. I knew he wouldn't hit me back. He just kept backing up blocking his face until he tripped and fell over the coffee table. In my rage I tried to kick him in the face, but he caught my foot and pushed me away and then hurried getting to his feet before I could try again. As I stumbled, I dropped my cell phone. Ray quickly scooped it off the floor. I tried to get it from him, and he threw it across the room. When I turned to get it, the nigga ran out the door.

I can't believe I fell for that shit. I felt so stupid, all I could do was drop down on the floor and cry my eyes out. "Fuck this shit. If he don't wanna be here, I got a place for him!" I picked up the phone and dialed 9-1-1. "If I can't have him, nobody will."

I explained to the officer that he had just jumped on me, and within minutes the police were knocking at the door. I was still crying uncontrollably when I let them in. One of the two officers talked to me while the other looked around at the mess I'd made of the living room.

"Can you tell me what happened here, ma'am?"

"Look, your hand is bleeding. Did your husband do that to you?" asked the female officer, cutting her partner off.

I hadn't noticed the small cut on my hand. It must have come from me acting a fool after he left. "Yeah, I think so." I don't know why I just lied, but it was too late; I couldn't take it back now.

"Okay, tell me what happened." She took over the questioning when she saw the cut.

"My ex-husband, Ray Jones, came over trying to get all lovey-dovey with me earlier today."

"What do you mean by lovey-dovey?" she asked as they both took notes of everything I was telling them.

"He. .. He. .. He was trying to kiss and hug on me, but I was upset with him for not coming home for a

14

week. So I told him no and to leave me alone, but he wouldn't, so I ignored him and finished helping my daughter with her homework. That's when he got mad and flipped the dining room table. I pointed to the table that I'd turned over in my rage. We started arguing, and then he took his daughter..."

"Now is this your child, or...?"

"No. She's my stepdaughter. She's been staying with me for about seven months. After he left, he started calling my phone repeatedly telling me that he's been drinking and I don't know how he can get when he's drinking."

Yeah, I was lying my ass off. I knew that nigga inside and out, but fuck him. He shouldn't have left me.

"Is that when he came back?"

"No. Later I had fell asleep on the couch, and that's when he woke me up punching me in the face." I dropped my head so they

couldn't get a look at my face. "He kept hitting me and yelling about me not answering the phone. That's when I tried to fight back and seen that he had a gun in his hand."

"Do you know what kind of gun it was?"

"I think it was a black 9 mm." I'm sure he had one like that around somewhere. "He started hitting me all over my body, yelling, 'Bitch, it's three o' clock in the morning. I'ma kill you. I know I'm going to jail, so I'ma kill you and them bitches on First Street since I ain't got nothing else to live for.'" I finished telling them all I could about Ray, except for where he was staying. I didn't need them to find his money and stuff when they locked him up. A bitch needed that to get by.

"Do you want to go to the hospital and get checked out?"

"No, I just want him caught before he come back and kill me." I held back my smile as the officers took pictures of me and the mess I'd made of the house.

After they were gone, I called Deidra and told her the same lies, but added that he was trying to make me tell him about her, so she would come over and protect me the way she had promised. Once she was on her way, I called my sisters and told them the story. I didn't want nobody fucking with him anymore. If he didn't want me, he couldn't have nothing! Deidra helped me clean the house up and then told me she was taking me to get a restraining order on him in the morning. I didn't wanna do all that, but I needed her to know that I was with her now and she was my "man," as Deidra liked to be referred to.

Chapter 3

WTF!

NOW THAT SHIT WAS crazy. After the last time I saw Donna, I got arrested, booked, tried, and sentenced for a domestic violence charge for something I didn't do. When I walked in that court room and saw that my lawyer and I were the only men in the room, I knew right then it was a hit. I didn't stand a chance at winning. The female ADA came to us with a deal for six months of probation and ninety days of domestic violence counseling if I plead guilty. My lawyer told me even though I didn't hit her, the fact that I told them that I pushed her off of me to get out of the house was enough for the judge to throw the book at me. Fuck that! I didn't do shit to her, so I told him to tell the ADA that

I'd plead no contest for the same deal, but not guilty. She agreed, the judge didn't. She hit me with thirty days in jail with childcare because she knew I had my daughter. A year probation, and I still had to do the damn DV counseling for ninety days.

I wasn't liking that county jail shit. It was a good thing that a nigga only had to do thirty days. Remember, I was supposed to get out every day to take care of my daughter. Yeah, that never happened. They kept telling me that when they went out to my address, no one was ever home. Dumbasses, I was in jail! That's why it wasn't nobody at my house. It's a good thing my daughter was with Dream, or them assholes would've had hell to pay for leaving a four-year-old-girl home alone for a whole fucking month, all because they wanted to play games with a nigga an' shit. It was just so hard for them to believe that I was a single dad.

I missed my baby like crazy. Even though I knew she was in good hands, I knew she was worried about me not answering my phone or nothing. I couldn't call her or anybody because like a lot of people, I depended on my phone to remember all the numbers I needed—all except close family members that pretty much had the same phone numbers for years. Yeah, I knew my baby's phone number, but I didn't have any money. I felt like a bum not having money on my books. The reason I didn't was that I thought I just would be walking in and out that day I went to court. So I emptied my pockets in my van before I went in so I could breeze through the metal detectors and pat downs that everyone was subject to when entering that part of the courthouse.

As you know, it wasn't my first time in, so I knew how to do my time. I got cool with a few guys on the cell block that hit me with the hygiene I needed to get by for the thirty days. I spent the time the way I always did when I went to jail. I played table games like spades, chess, and dominoes when I was out in the dayroom.

And when I was locked down for the night I worked out and wrote until I fell off into dreamland.

I wish I could say the time went by fast, but it was the muthafuckin' opposite. I think it was the longest thirty days in my life. I wrote a whole novel while I was there. I was so happy when that officer unlocked my cell and told me to pack up at 2:00 a.m., and I was shocked when the cashier handed me $20 cash and a check for another $80. I thought it was a mistake, but I didn't tell her that. Hell nawl,

I wasn't giving it back. Her bad. Hell, before I got a little money, I had planned on walking to my sister's house since it was the closest to downtown. But since I had money, I asked one of the guys that I was released with if I could pay him the $20 to take me to Mica's. I knew she would be awake because she worked third shift and could never sleep on her days off. I got another surprise when I walked out of jail. My uncle Curt was there waiting on me.

"I thought you might need a ride, you bastard." He smiled, happy to see me.

"Hell yeah. Get me the hell away from here." I let the guy I paid keep the money. Hell, it wasn't my money anyway.

"Why didn't you call nobody?" Curt asked once I was in his van.

"I didn't have no money, and I didn't wanna be begging niggas for three-way calls an' shit."

"What you mean you didn't have no money? I put a bill on your books when you didn't come back from court that day."

"Well, they didn't give me a receipt, so I didn't know. I just thought that bitch in there fucked up when she gave a nigga that." I noticed that we were heading toward his house. "Unc, can you drop me off at Mica's? I'll have her drop me off at the house later."

"Shit, bastard, you can drop yourself off. I got your van parked at my house. Look in the glovebox and get the keys." He pointed. "I knew you were gonna need it ASAP when you got out, plus I didn't want shit to happen to it just sitting outside the house with nobody there."

"Good looking. I knew somebody still loved me," I joked as we rounded the corner and pulled in behind my van.

When I got in my van I ran through my playlist and put on "Touch Down" by Yo Gotti. I let it bang loud on my way to Mica's. Just like I knew she would be, she was home watching TV. She gave me a hug and then kissed a nigga like I'd been gone for years. She explained that she didn't know I was in jail until the day before when Uncle Curt told her. I couldn't focus on nothing but that sexy body of hers under the oversized T-shirt she was wearing. But I didn't want to hit it and run like she didn't mean nothing to me, so we just sat and talked. I let her know that I loved her, and then it was time for the kids to go to school, so I left to go see my baby girl.

I wanted to surprise her when she walked out of the house to head to her bus stop. When I pulled up in front of Dream's house,

Pooh was just walking out. She was so happy to see me that she started crying. I got out of the van, and she ran and leaped into my arms. I held onto my baby tight, and all of my thoughts of vengeance for the time I had to spend away from her went away. Well, all of my thoughts of doing any physical harm. That was it. Fuck Donna! She wasn't getting another dime from me. So she had better made that little stuff she took from me count.

After I dropped my baby off at school and promised that I'd be there to pick her up at the end of the day, I made my way to the phone store to pay my phone bills so I could get back on my grind. But not until I went back over Mica's and took a nap because I had been up over twenty-four hours already. As soon as my phones were reconnected I got a call from Didi asking me to come see her later when she got off work. I agreed and then changed my mind and went home to take that nap. But before I did, I logged onto my Facebook to check in with my people and let them know where I'd been and to shoot the shit with them until I fell asleep.

Sleep didn't last long before the constant ringing of my two phones ended my much-needed rest. I had to meet up with my nigga so we could hit the highway to re-up. It's good to have a nigga you can count on when you're down to hold things down.

"Assa, get your lazy ass out the pussy, nigga. It's time to zoom. I'm out, and we need to go. I see the van out here, so I know you in there."

"Yeah, I'm here. Just give me a sec." I got up and jumped in

the shower quickly to wash that jail off me, then dressed and ran outside to meet him.

"You driving, nigga," he said, already sitting in the passenger's seat. "I heard from ol' Doc what happened to you. That shit was foul as hell, my nigga. I be seeing Donna's ass riding around like she didn't do shit wrong." He talked while smoking his blunt.

As he filled me in on all that was going on, I thought of how I was finna tell him that I was about to be done with the drug shit. I didn't want to keep risking being taken away from my babies again. Yeah, right after them next two flips, I was done. I was gonna put my time and money back into selling my used cars and try to make it from there. I felt good about my chances because I no longer had Donna and her issues to deal with. So, yeah, I knew

I'd be good once I got all the money up I needed to step away from it all.

WHEN IS FAR ENOUGH?

Adequate provocation means sufficient provocation to cause complete loss of self-control in an ordinary person. That is an extreme mental disturbance or emotional state. It is in which one's ability to exercise judgment is overcome to the extent that one acts uncontrollably. It is the highest degree of anger, rage, or exasperation.

Chapter 4

Deidra

IT WAS TIME FOR me to set another exa-mple and let niggas know I wasn't the one to be fucked with. That silly muthafucka thought he could put his hands on my bitch and wasn't gonna have to face the music behind it. The fool had another thing coming.

"What it do, fam! Let's have a seat over here," I greeted my folks, Dink, as soon as he walked through the door of the bar. I didn't know the nigga he brought with him, so I told him to have a seat at the bar and asked my sister to give him a drink on me.

"Say now, Blacky, I like free drinks too."

"Man, you know you good, but let me holla at you

about why I called you down here first."

"This shit sound serious. What's good?" he asked
as we sat down.

"I need to make a nigga respect my gangsta. He
need to know it ain't sweet this way, feel me?"

"Shit, cuz, all you gotta do is point 'em out and it's
a done deal." He drew his gun and placed it on the
table to show me he

was ready for whatever.

"Fool, put that away before sis get on your ass."
He did. "I just want y'all to hurt the nigga, not kill
him. I fuck with the nigga kids an' shit. Anyway, the
nigga holdin'. He move weight on both sides."

"Oh, hell yeah! A nigga need a good lick like a
muthafucka right now. Who is this nigga?"

"It's this bitch I'm fucking on ex-husband. His
name Asa or some shit. Do you know him?"

"Naw, and it don't matter if I did because we're
family and you know that means fuck the rest."

"Fo sho. I don't know where the nigga lay his
head. All my bitch told me is that he kept all of his
real cash and work somewhere other than her crib.
But I ended up following him one day to a house
over on the corner of Wright Street. I'm not sure if
that's his spot or what. I asked ol' girl about it. I told

her that he followed me when I left her house and then turned off over there. She said that's the nigga's mama's crib where he keeps most of his cars."

"What kinda whips he drive?"

"Shit, all kinda shit, but he mostly be in a gray-and-blue Chevy van or a orange-and-red MC."

"Is you talking about the one I seen parked up the street from here a few times?" he asked, pushing his dreads out of his face and then putting back on his Milwaukee cap.

"Yeah, why? Do you know somebody down there?" I wanted to see if he knew Donna or her daughter.

"Naw, I had thought about stripping that nigga myself. He be riding by hisself all the time, right?"

"Shit. The hell if I know. But my bitch told me. . ." I looked over at his guy talking to my sister. "Hey, tell your guy to stay here and come ride with me right quick so I can show you the house."

Yeah, I know I got trust issues, but that's what keeps me ahead of the game. Once we were in my car I pulled out a sack of weed and a blunt. "Here, nigga, roll up." I passed it to him and then pulled off and explained, "I rode through here a few times to see just how much the nigga be over here. I seen him talking to a bunch of young niggas that I know who be out here hustlin'. So I drove down on one of them and bought a sack from them just to see if it was the same weed I got from my bitch."

Dink took a pull off the blunt and passed it to me. "Fam, this that shit! If that's what the nigga holdin', hell,

we need that."

"You know the deal, cuz. We bust everything down the middle," I remined him as I pulled over up the street from Donna's ex mother-in-law's house so we could get the layout of the spot. After a few minutes, I seen Assa walking out of the alley. "Look, there he go right there, and the lil nigga he talking to is the same one I got the sack from the other day."

"I think that lil nigga sitting on the Caddy must be holding

work for him or something. I gotta lil bitch I can put on that nigga." Dink hit the weed again and then flashed his gold-toothed smile. "Pull off. I'ma see what it do over these ways later."

I dropped him off at his car where his guy was waiting for him because Dink had called and told him that we were on our way back. I thought about something he had said about putting a bitch on Donna's ex. Donna did mention that he was a pussy hound and be tricking off on bitches left and right so they wouldn't tell on him. If that's true I had a hoe just for his ass. Who knew, I might get lucky and get the fool-ass nigga to take her where he kept his stash. I kept this idea to myself and let cuz do his thang while I did mine.

An hour later I walked out of the bar going to make a few runs. As I drove past the alley, I saw Donna's ex's van stopped in the middle of the alley behind her house. He was talking to her kids from what I could see, but I kept watching to see if he went in the house. I promise you I was gonna beat that bitch's ass if she was still fucking with him behind my back. I pulled my gun out from under the seat thinking about going down there and pistol whipping his bitch ass for what he had done to her and telling him to stay away from my bitch. "Yeah, the nigga needs to know that I ain't hard to find since he looking for me an' shit."

But he never got out of the van, and as soon as the kids had gotten what they wanted from him, he pulled off. I pulled in front of the alley's exit, blocking him from leaving, and pointed my gun

at him from out my window. He didn't flinch or try to back up or nothing. In fact, he turned up his music and shook his head. "What the fuck? Do this nigga think he bulletproof or some shit?" I put my gun away and sped off because it was too many eyes out, but I knew he got the message. "Yeah, I gotta get that nigga. I'ma put the lil chick Star on him. I know her fine ass can get his ass. I'ma learn that fool to respect me."

"Hey. bae! I was just thinking about you," Donna answered.

I called Donna to see where she was after seeing her truck wasn't in its parking place. That didn't mean shit. Donna's ass still could be in the house or in the van with him and had let her sister use her truck to throw me off.

"Yeah? Where you at?" I could hear females laughing and talking in her background. One of the voices sounded like Donna's sister, Neek.

"I'm on my way to the mall with Neek and her friend. Why, you need me to do something?"

"No, I'm good. I just seen your husband at your house."

"One of them kids must've called him over there because it wasn't me. I ain't been at the house since like ten this morning."

"Bitch, don't let me find out you lying and make me have to go upside your head."

"Whoa, I'm not, bae. You can come up to Mayfair

right now and see for yourself."

"I don't got time for all that. I was just playin', but you need to hurry up and get up out that house. I don't want that nigga knowing where I lay my head."

"Oh, I will. I got to go look at one in the morning that I found in the rent assistance office when I went in to talk about why the police was at the house."

"What you tell 'em?"

"That my ex-husband had found out where I lived and came over trying to get back with me. And when I refused, he attacked me. When I got finished with my story, the bitch put me at the top of the list and gave me a few places to look at. Don't worry, bae, I'm on my shit."

"Okay, that's what I needed to hear." I pulled up in front of my other bitch's crib. "I gotta go in there and hit her off so she'll stop blowing my phone the fuck up. "I'ma get up with you later. I gotta handle something right quick," I told her as I got out, promising Donna that I'd try to see her later tonight after I closed the club. Then found the key I needed to let myself in the house and ended the call.

Chapter 5

Damn Stick-Up Kids

IT WAS EARLY MORNING, and I'd just dropped my baby off at school and seen that I needed gas, so I pulled the van into the gas station on Appleton and Center, across from Big Bill's Used Cars. I was glad the station wasn't packed, so I could run in and out. I needed to get home and change before I met up with Ty to hit the highway. Yep, you guessed right if you guessed it was re-up time again. Anyway, as I walked out of the station, two cars pulled onto the lot. One was a newer-model Jag with a flashy nigga driving it. I thought it was too early for all that, but that's new money for you. When he got out of the car flashing a big wad of cash, I thought for sure the car full of youngstas that parked in front of me was gonna rob him.

They fooled the hell outta me, and boy was I wrong. The next time I looked up from my phone I was surrounded with a gun a few inches from my face. There was nothing I could do either. I was caught between my van and the gas pump with two wild-looking young niggas, one on each side of me.

"Nigga, you know what it is! Run that shit willingly, or I can take it off your body!" barked the dread head with the gun in front of me. "Don't look at me! Look at the ground. Fuck that, get on the ground, bitch-ass nigga!"

"I'm not getting on the ground. Y'all can have this lil shit I got. It ain't no need to shoot me for it." I pulled out the wad of cash I had in my pocket. It totaled over $3,400. The reason I had that much on me that early was because I'd served my guy before I went out to Didi's the night before for some awesome breakup sex, and then this mess happened. I ain't gonna lie to you, I wanted to ask them why they was robbing me instead of the flashy fool? But I didn't hate.

The goon to the left of me tried to open the van's door, but it was locked. My doors locked automatic-ally when I got in and out of it. I knew he was finna try to take the keys, so I dropped them and kicked them under the van. When he saw what I'd done, he tried to hit me, but I dodged the blow and deflected it, causing him to hit the pump. I was in full fight mode, but before I could get to it, I heard the flashy nigga yell, "What the fuck!"

That caused the robbers to flee back to their maroon Buick and speed off. Mr. Flashy asked me if I was alright once he returned from wherever he had run to when he saw the gun. I told him I was good and then crawled under my van and retrieved the keys. Once I had them, I finished filling up my tank and then got in and pulled

off. As I headed home I wondered how long they had been following me because I knew it wasn't just some random robbery. I thought I remembered seeing that Buick make a U-turn up the street but didn't pay it no mind. I couldn't get a good look at their faces because they had their shirts pulled over their mouths and their hats down low.

I went on with my day like nothing ever happened. Hell, there wasn't anything I could do but accept the loss and thank the Lord it was all I had lost. I told my brother about the robbery, and he went over it again and again as we left and returned to the state. Once back from the trip, I hit the kitchen right away so I could catch the cash on my line. Once I had all my orders ready, we hit the streets going our separate ways. Ty had his grind to get to, and I had mine.

As I was finishing up my last few drops, both of my phones started ringing. They had been ringing for some time because I had a few missed calls that I didn't hear because of the music I was riding to.

"I know you missed me, but damn, can a nigga get some down time?" I answered, muting the radio.

"Assa, this Tonya. I didn't know who else to call, so I called you."

"Is everything alright? Where Money at?"

"He right here, but I don't wanna say too much over the phone. So you need to get down here ASAP."

"Enough said, I'll be there in like five minutes," I promised and then ended the call.

I made a U-turn and then headed down to the east side to see what was going on. I was already strapped because of the robbery that morning. The block was quiet and still when I made it there. When I got out of the car and walked into the yard, the first thing I noticed was the blood on the ground. I clutched the Sig .357 inside the pocket of my hoody as I followed the trail to the back of the house. There I noticed the back door was busted and hastily boarded up. I ran back to the front door and banged on it until Tonya peeked out the window.

"Bro, I'm glad you're here. Money won't let me take him to the hospital for his head. It's bleeding bad and won't stop," she quickly explained as I hurried inside.

"What the fuck happened here?" I asked, making my way into the kitchen, where I found Money holding a blood-soaked towel to the big gash in his head.

"We got robbed. I'll let him tell you what happened. See if you can get him to go to the hospital."

"Bitch, I said I ain't going to no muthafuckin' hospital! Them bitches gonna call the police, and what we finna tell 'em?" He took a pull off the blunt he was holding. "Big bro, them bitch-ass niggas hit me with they gun and split my shit open for nothing." He removed the towel so I could see the gash.

My nigga was hurting, both inside and out. But first things first, we had to stop the bleeding, and then we could address his pride.

"Man, don't you wanna go to the hospital and let

them fix you up? We can tell 'em you fell off a ladder drinking or some shit. I'll go with y'all."

He shook his head no.

"Fuck that! Bro, didn't you tell me that you had to patch niggas up like this in the Feds? So, yeah, I want you to do this shit so we can get out there and find them niggas that robbed me."

"Money, you trippin'. If you're sure you want me to do it, I will, but it's gonna hurt like a muthafucka," I warned him, trying to talk him out of having me do it.

"I said do it, bruh. I can take a lick just like any other nigga can. I put that on the five I can!" He slapped his chest as he made his oath. "Niggas gonna bleed like me for this shit!"

Money spoke with true conviction. I knew he meant every word he was saying. I also knew his pride was hurt to have his wife see him all beat up like he was. I looked at Tonya, who looked like a scared little girl standing behind him.

"Okay, let's do this," I gave in. Then I barked out a list of all of the things I needed to stitch him up.

She didn't say another word and just quickly gathered all she had and brought it to me. I think she was more curious to see me do it than anything at this point. I took the peroxide and soaked the gash while Money held his head over the kitchen sink. Once it was clean I told Tonya to hold ice on it to numb the area.

"Money, this shit is finna be cold, and it's still gonna hurt like hell, but you gotta take it because this needle gonna hurt worse without it being numbed first," I explained, standing at the table soaking thread in peroxide and then the needle after burning it to clean it.

"Assa, do you need anything else before I go, because I can't watch this," she admitted.

"I might need you to hold his hands down when I get started."

"What! I'm good," Money said just as the doorbell rang, saving Tonya from the task.

"I'll get it."

"Tonya, keep 'em up there. I don't want them seeing me like this here," he yelled behind her. "I'm good, bro. Let's do this."

"Okay. Well sit on your hands and don't move. I don't wanna go too deep." He did like I said and let me give him some homemade stitches.

When I finished I let him admire my handiwork before Tonya covered it with some kinda ointment from their cheap first-aid kit. I asked Money to tell me what happened from beginning to end because it was crazy. First me that morning, and then him later the same day. He told the three of us the story. Tonya's best friend had come over to show support in whatever way she could. They were the ones that started cleaning up around the house.

"I had just made it here to pick up some more work because I had a few moves to make."

"Did you see any cars following you?" I asked.

"Nope. I look for shit like that all the time. I didn't see nothing out of place when I dropped here," he answered, and then took a sip of his beer. "I used the back door so I could run right downstairs and put the orders together. But as soon as I turned the corner, they put a AK or some shit in my face."

"So you know what they look like?"

"Nope. One had on one of them half masks with his hat pulled down low, and the other one had one of them hoodies with the skull face that zipped all the way up." He answered then waited for my next question. I kept it to myself and let him go on with the story. "Big bruh, I couldn't do shit because I didn't know if Tonya was in the house or not, and I didn't want her to come out and get hurt." He looked over at his wife. "I just did what the nigga with the gun in my face said. He pushed me into the house, where his partner was waiting. As soon as he seen me, he slapped me with his gun and told me that he wanted it all. I didn't want to ask them shit about my girl because if they had her they would've used her, plus I didn't want them to look for her just in case she was somewhere hiding." He took another sip of his beer and then went on. "I didn't see no blood on the floor nowhere, so I didn't worry all that much, but I still did what they told me to do. Man, bruh, I thought I was finna die after I gave them the money and work that was in the safe. They made me get on my knees, and then the next thing I know the bitch-ass nigga hit me in the back of the head with his gun. It must've knocked me the fuck out, because the next thing I remember was Tonya holding me, crying."

"So you were in the house when all this shit happened?" I asked her.

"Yeah, but I was upstairs asleep. I didn't hear nothing," Tonya answered, looking ashamed for not being there to help her man.

"Do y'all think anybody saw them kick the door in?"

"I don't know, maybe the old lady in the back

house next door seen something. She always looking out her windows over here," she told me.

"Yeah, maybe she seen them before they put their masks on," her friend Megan said, wanting to help.

I knew getting the plate number was useless unless they decided to call the police, and I doubted that. The police were going to ask way too many questions that they didn't have answers for.

"Let's go ask her," I told Money, getting up and heading toward the door without waiting for him to agree.

Just like they said, the elderly white woman was baking pies or something that smelled good and sweet. She told us that she didn't see anybody break into the house or she would have called the police, but she did see some guys with braids getting in a little red car when she came out to go to the store for some eggs. I thanked her, cutting the rest of her story off about the guy at the store, and went back into Money's yard. I told him that I thought it was the same guys that robbed me.

"I think they followed me over here a different day and then just came back today after they got that lil cash off of me this morning."

"And you don't know who these niggas is?" Money asked, ready to kill someone for what was done to him.

"Nope, but I'ma find out. Everybody talks, especially when it's money up for grabs." We went back in the house, and I asked him if they took everything.

"Nawl, I don't keep a lot of cash here. We put it in the bank."

I ain't gonna lie, I was surprised at his honesty. I told Money that I would straighten him out on my next flip and allow him to get his work at cost because I felt like what happened to him was because of me. When I checked the time, I saw that it was time to go pick up my baby from school.

"Here, keep this on you just in case. I gotta go handle something right fast. I'ma holla at them brothas on Wells and see if they know who these niggas is and put 'em up on shit," I told him, handing him the gun before I rushed out of the house.

On the way to the school, I wondered what was going on. I guessed it had to be someone that knew me behind it. Well, that knew a little about me anyway. I stayed looking in my rearview mirrors for anything that looked out of place. I felt vulnerable without the Sig on me, but I didn't need to have it if

I got pulled over for speeding. I had niggas on my team that'd snatch a nigga's kids just to get to him, so I knew if they thought this way, so did others.

Just the thought of something like that had me really racing to get to my daughter's school to pick her up.

As I drove, I called a few of my guys and told them to be on the lookout for the maroon Buick Park Avenue and called a meeting so we could talk about everything and come up with a good way to handle it. At school, my daughter and her friends were standing out front playing around when I pulled up. I was glad she was safe, but I still watched every car that drove by before I pulled up next to her, just to be on the safe side. Once she was in the van, I told her that she was going to have to take the school bus for a few days because I was going to be very busy with work. Pooh was cool with it. She was looking for a reason to hang out with her new friends more anyway.

After I dropped her off at Dream's, I headed to the garage to get out of the van. I swapped it for my Chevy Tahoe and then went back down to Money's spot where everyone was gonna meet up to talk about what was going on.

Chapter 6

Deidra

LASHANN'S OL' BUSYBODY ass was on me about Donna while counting the money the club made that night at the same time.

"Deidra, that bitch is crazy. I can't be having her up in here acting a fool over you like that." She paused to finish off her drink. "You know she drunk outta your glass in front of Ralonda to start some shit with her, right?"

"Yeah, I know she did." I smiled at the thought of how sexy that shit was. "Sis, you know I ain't with all that drama shit. I'ma leave the bitch alone since she can't respect me like that. If she can't respect my other bitches, then that's disrespecting me.

Donna knew her place when we started fucking around."

"Yeah, but now that that nigga she was fucking with gone, she want you all to herself."

"Yeah, I know."

I took a deep pull off of the blunt I was holding as I helped her clean the place up for tomorrow. We closed for the night, so it was just the two of us cleaning up. My sister was bitching about

Donna and her sister Neek. They'd come in tonight and gotten some shit started with this other bitch I'd been fucking with for a while now. Me and Ralonda had a long-term on-and-off-again relationship. I knew what she would do if things got tough. Donna, not so much. So to kill all of the bullshit, I was gonna break it off with Donna. Hell, when you think about it, the bitch really didn't have shit for me now that her husband wasn't fucking with her like that. I could get pussy anywhere. I had a couple of bitches I could bust down on sight, anytime, anyplace.

So I really didn't need her and them badass kids of hers for nothing. I'd be lying if I said I didn't feel a little something for her. It was just not enough for her to be taking me through bullshit. I would holla at her, and if she wasn't talking right I'd be gone. "La, is you going down to Potawatomi when you leave here?"

"Yeah, I'm feeling lucky tonight!" she sang, doing her little happy dance. "I'll be done here in a few. Here, you hold on to this. I don't wanna put it all in them machines down there. You know how I can get when I get going," she said, handing me the currency bag.

"Didn't you just say you was feeling lucky? What happen to that?" I asked, stuffing the bag into the pocket of my black hoody. "Oh, I'm feeling lucky, just not stupid."

We laughed as we walked out of the bar together. I stood watch while she locked the door and gate. Then we got into our cars and went our separate ways. Lashann was on her way to gamble, and I was on my way to get some fire head from Donna and then check her ass for acting a fool tonight.

"What it do, cuz?" I asked, answering my phone just as I made the turn onto North Avenue.

"Shit, shit, just lurking as always." He chuckled. "I just seen the van of that nigga you put me on parked over on Michigan. What do you know about that area?"

"Shit, nothing. I ain't really been seeing that nigga lately. I thought he switched up cars again?"

"Oh, well don't trip. I'm finna make it do what it do. I'll holla back."

"Fo sho. You be careful, fam. He bound to be on point after the way y'all been on his ass," I warned him, coming to a stop at the light on Fond du Lac and North.

"Fam, I'm good. All I need is my banger and a full clip for me to come out on top. You just be ready to count this cash."

The punk hung up on me before I could finish talking to him. So I said fuck it and texted Donna telling her that I would be there in a few minutes and asking her if she needed anything from the store before I got there. She responded saying all she needed was me, so I stopped at the gas station on Twenty-Seventh and Capital. I ran in and grabbed two Red Bulls and a box of blunts and then headed straight to her place to fuck the shit outta her for the night.

A short time later, Donna met me at the door in a little dark blue robe with nothing on under it. As soon as we were behind the closed doors of her bedroom she let the robe fall to the floor, simultaneously taking my hand and placing it between her warm thighs.

"See, daddy, it's ready for you. I know you mad at me for what I did, but I love you, and I don't know what came over me. I'm sorry, daddy. Let me make it up to you," she begged.

"I should've slapped the hell outta your ass for disrespecting me like that." I pulled my hand from hers and then stepped back and slapped her across the face hard. "Bitch, don't you ever in your life do that shit again!" I warned her. I remembered her telling me that her ex didn't put his hands on her even when she knew she needed her ass kicked. I guess this was one of those times. Hell, her reaction to the blow could be the reason I stopped fucking with her.

"I won't. I'm sorry, bae, I don't wanna fight," she told me, holding her face with tears in her eyes.

"Come here!" I ordered her as I took her in my arms and kissed her hard.

She started undressing me, and I let her push me backward until I fell back on the bed. She got down between my thighs and went to work. Donna sucked me until I squirted in her face, and then she slid her warm body up mine to let me taste myself

48

off of her lips before she put her sweet pussy in my mouth. We went back and forth for what seemed like hours. When we took a smoke break, I told her that I would be spending New Years with Ralonda because of the way she acted in the bar.

"Can I at least stop in there to see you, bae?" she asked, taking a sip of my Red Bull.

"As long as you don't start no shit. If you do I'ma beat that ass for real and we done. Do you understand me?" She agreed just as my phone started playing my cousin's ringtone.

It was a text telling me to call him when I had time. I put it off until later because it was late, and if it was important the nigga would've called. He might just wanna tell me he got some more cash for me that he took off of another one of Assa's guys. So, yeah, it could wait until I was away from Donna.

Chapter 7

They're Never Around When I Need Them

MONTHS AFTER PUTTING THE word out about the robbers, things slowed down a bit. I went through a few more incidents that I believed to be because of them, but I still didn't know who they were. But I had pulled back from the streets a bit more so I could be more of a caretaker to my daughter and a better partner to Mica.

Mica had proven herself to be more than just good sex when a nigga was feeling lonely. When you really looked at her you'd see that she was a hard-working single mother. Yeah, she was a little crazy at times, but I knew I gave her every right to get on me the way she did when she got crazy. The most important thing that I loved about her was the way she was with my daughter and the way Pooh responded to her. I don't remember if I told you this before, but Mica had three boys of her own. And like most women with all boys she longed for a daughter. So Pooh was the answer to her prayers in a way. But Mica could've had one of her own had she not decided to abort my baby without giving me a chance to decide the child's fate with her. She told me the reason for her not having the baby was because she did not believe that I would be there for her and the child because of Donna. I was hurt after the abortion. Honestly, I still am. I have this emptiness in my heart now that Autumn is gone, but I understand. We're good now. Hell, if I got lucky I would knock her up again. Insha Allah (if God wills).

The Christmas holiday came up fast. I didn't celebrate it really myself, but I enjoyed watching my kids. I believed they all enjoyed the things they got and just having me there with them. Pooh gave me a hand-carved Native American wooden box, and my goddaughter gave me one of my all-time favorite movies on DVD, I Am Legend. Like I said, I did it for the kids.

Anyway, after the holiday, I was chilling at Mica's place with the kids and her eighteen-year-old niece, Sparkle, and her boyfriend. Only Mica's oldest son and my daughter were there with us. The other two were still with their dad for the Christmas school break. Mica went out to a party with her sisters and a bunch of other family members. They had invited me, but I wasn't in a club mood that night. I just chilled with the kids watching a couple of movies before going into the bedroom to get some quiet time. I also wanted to talk some shit on Facebook.

It was a little after one in the morning when I heard the alarm on my van go off. My daughter had the keys, so I let her deal with it.

"Daddy! Daddy, it's a minivan crashed into the van!"

"What the fuck!" I said more to myself than to her as I raced out of the house to see how bad it was. When I got out there I found an abandoned stolen Dodge minivan T-boned into the side of my van. I was past pissed the fuck off. Sparkle called the police for me while I got in the Dodge and backed it off of mine. I needed to see in front of it so I could better assess the damage. I was glad that it was nothing more than a small dent and scratch. The Dodge had hit it just enough to set off the alarm.

When that realization hit me I, right away, scanned the area to see if it was a setup because the scene looked fishy to me.

I got my answer when I spotted the maroon Buick parked almost a block away from us. It looked to be a car full, from what I could see from where I was standing. Before I could decide on what to do next, a black Jeep Compass came around the corner and stopped in front of me and my daughter. It cut us off from the house so the others couldn't really see what was going on from the porch. I gripped my gun that I had grabbed on my way out and stuffed in my back pocket. I pushed my daughter behind me to shield her with my body just in case I had to pull the gun.

"Hey, fam, is this your van?" the passenger of the Jeep asked me out the window.

"Yeah, why?" I saw there were a few more people in the Jeep with him, but I couldn't make them out because of the dark tint on the windows. I still never took my eye off of the back door.

At this time, the white people that lived across from Mica came out of the house to see what was going on in front of their house.

"Pull off," he told the driver, and they pulled off

and then stopped a few feet away once they saw the old woman's family getting into their car to leave. "Say, fam, is that your bitch?"

"Nope, my daughter," I said. Then I wished I hadn't for her safety, but it was too late, and they drove off, so, oh well.

"Daddy, here come the police."

"Okay, go on the porch with them," I told her, sending her onto the porch with Sparkle and the others. I quickly eased my gun out of my pocket and placed it on the floor inside my van just in case the police wanted to get on some bullshit with me. I don't have to tell you that many of the officers in the MPD don't play well with us on the north side. But I did all that for nothing because they went the other way. They weren't the ones we called. To see a lot of police in that area was kinda the norm, so I just waited for the next squad to come.

But before that happened both the Jeep and the Buick came back. I hadn't even noticed that the car had pulled off until it was parking back up the block from where I was standing. The Jeep stopped in front of me again. Only this time I was defenseless because I'd locked my gun in the van, but I didn't let them know that.

"Now what?" I asked the passenger, getting a good look at his face this time.

"Hey, folks, this a tough nigga!" he told the thugs in the Jeep with him.

Then he pulled his gun and the back door of the jeep open, but before his guy could get out or anything else could go down, the old lady saved my black ass again by coming out to be nosey some more. "Hey, I called the cops for you. They should be here in a few," she informed me as she walked toward me holding a hot cup of coffee or something.

"Okay, thanks!" I was grinning as I turned back to the guys in the jeep. "She said the police should be on their way here, so y'all might wanna just leave," I told him, staring him down and keeping my eye on the gun in his hand that he was now holding just below the window. They pulled off again and so did the car.

"They shouldn't be speeding through here like that," the old woman told me.

"Yeah, miss, I don't know what's going on, but you should go in the house because they got guns and they keep coming back for something." She did as I said, telling me that she was going to call the police again. I told the kids to go in the house and not to come out for nothing. I was planning to trap the fools if they came back, by hiding in my van and jumping out blasting if they tried to run up in the house. I had my gun and was getting ready for them, when Mica called me and told me she was pulling up to the house. I kinda told her what was going on, but not too much on the phone.

A few minutes later she was pulling up, and also at that time so was the Jeep, but I didn't see the Buick this time. They didn't say anything to me this time. One of the guys in the back got out and jumped in the Dodge and took off behind the Jeep. Now who does that? It was a fucking stolen van. Just leave it and go, but not if you don't want the police to get your fingerprints off of it, you don't.

As soon as they drove away, the fools in the Buick came driving by waving their guns in the air like I was supposed to be scared or something. Hell, they were lucky that Mica was standing by my side, or I would've given them a real reason to be speeding away. The police finally pulled up five minutes or so later. I shook my head, but, hey, that's how they treat us black folks. Anyhow, I explained to them what went down with the help of my nosey neighbor. They made a report and then left. Then, like ten minutes later, they called to inform me that they found the Dodge minivan a few blocks away and that it was stolen from just up the street from Mica's place.

I didn't get much sleep that night. Later that day I put my guys up on both of the vehicles and let them know what I thought was going on. Since they now knew where my girl lived, I had my guys ride through here and there to keep an eye out for trouble. I also made it my business to come to her house every night to make sure she was safe. I needed to show them fools that I really wasn't scared of them. I knew they didn't know who I was or they wouldn't have been on what they were on with me. But then again, these young niggas crazy these days. Well, if they were smart they wouldn't be too quick to run up in Mica's house with me there knowing that I'm onto them.

I decided to use this time to spread the word that I was done with the game. I had lost a handful of my team to the prisons and graveyards in those few months prior, so it was time to give it a break. Believe it or not, Mica said she was ready to tough it out with me. She really seemed to believe in me, and that's what I needed to get back focused on bringing my dream of happiness to life. I really wasn't sure if she was the one that I was supposed to be with, but she seem to be willing, so why not give it a try?

Chapter 8

It All Falls Down

HAPPY NEW YEAR! I made it through ano-ther one, Al-Hamdu Lillah (Praise be to God). I felt that year was gonna be my year. Yeah, my time to shine the way I really wanted to.

I brought the year in just hanging out with the girl and the kids. I was really starting to feel like I was where I was supposed to be. I had the love of my kids, and not one, but two strong women in my corner. Most of all, I had a fresh start in my life that I planned to make the best of. I remember getting the call from Donna's sister, Tameka, asking me if I could give her and her son a ride over to her friend's house on the south side. She also needed to borrow a few bucks because she had overdone it bringing in the New Year the night before. Since Mica had some running of her own to do, I agreed to give her a ride. Donna's sister Tameka had always been my girl. She was my friend before I met her sister, and, yes, you guessed right, she was the one who introduced us. But what Donna had done had nothing to do with her, so we were good.

After dropping, her off I decided to stop by my mom's place to check on it because she had been spending a lot of time traveling with her boyfriend lately. I wanted to make sure things were good just in case they took off without telling me or something. I drove while Pooh sat on my side chopping it up on Facebook with her friends on her phone. I came to a stop at a red light on Thirty-Fifth and North Avenue, and when I looked to my right, I spotted no other than the bitch-ass niggas that had been on my ass. They were standing right beside the black Jeep Compass talking to none other than ol' Deidra, my ex-wife's lover.

Yeah, I'd found out that Donna was fucking around with a female from her kids, her mother, and Dream, more or less. None of them was happy about the way shit went down between Donna and me, nor were they feeling Deidra. I didn't give a fuck who she was fucking as long as she was leaving me the fuck alone. But I saw that that wasn't the case. All of the bullshit that had been going on with me and mines was because of these fools. As soon as the light changed, I sped off before I got out and caught a new case or worse. Plus I didn't want to get my baby hurt if something did happen.

I was so mad that I forgot about checking on my mother's house. I just needed to get as far away from there as I could, fast. When I snapped back, I was at my cousin's house out by the Falls. I told Chocolate about everything that had been going on.

"Cuz, I know that bitch ain't that stupid. You should try talking to Donna and see what she knows about it, or better yet, because all the bitch gonna do is lie, you should talk to her sister.

The one she be with all the time. Y'all still cool, right?" Chocolate talked while rolling herself a nice blunt.

"Yeah, we good, but Neek ain't finna do shit but lie for her ass. Hell, the only one I can talk to that'll tell me the truth is her little sister, Tee. I doubt if she knows anything because Donna been shitting on her ever since she found out that she was on the pipe."

"You still should try to holla at her. If she say them bitches do got something to do with the stuff that's been going on with you, then come get me. You know I'll beat a muthafucka's ass about mines!"

We talked about what her and her wannabe Megan Good lookalike friend did for New Years. Chocolate also set me up a Skype page as I tried to make up my mind on what to do about Donna and her people. By the time Chocolate was finished showing me how to use the site and smoking her second blunt, I'd decided to take her advice and try to talk to Donna's sister. If I could get Tee to call Donna and have her call me so we could talk, that would tell me if she had anything to do with the shit or not.

When I left my cousin's crib, I dropped my daughter off at my best friend's house for the night. I called Donna myself, but as always, she didn't answer. I knew I couldn't go to her place to talk to her face-to-face because she had moved without telling me where. I'd only found out from my uncle a few days afterward when he told me that he saw a moving truck in front of the old house. Anyway, I texted Tee and asked her to call me when she got off work. I talked to Tameka about it over the phone, and she did confirm that Deidra was known for setting people up and robbing niggas. She told me that she also sold weed. Now I knew what happened to the shit I had at that house. Tameka went on to tell me that she didn't like Deidra because of the way she treated the kids.

I told her about the time when the boys called me to pick them up saying that they just wanted to hang out with me, but when I picked them up to go see a movie they told me how much they didn't like Deidra and were talking about breaking out her car windows and then running away from home if I said they couldn't come live with me. They even reminded me of the promise I'd made to them, to always be there for them. I told them not to do anything silly and I would talk to their mother about it. But I'd never gotten around to calling Donna about it. She ended up calling me talking about having them placed in a boys home or some shit like that because they were being disrespectful. I laughed on the inside but begged her not to do that and asked her to allow them to come stay with me for a few days so I could get their minds right.

I'd been in a few group homes growing up and knew firsthand the abuse that went on in them. When I was young, I thought I was on top of the world because I was fucking an older female staff member. Yeah, she used to sneak in my room in the early hours to give me blowjobs and teach me how to fuck her until she came hard. It was fun until it wasn't. I was young, and now I see that it was rape.

That bitch was like thirty-plus and I was only like thirteen or fourteen. Anyway, Donna told me that she would think about it after she gave their deadbeat dads a chance to step up for them. I told her good luck with that. These were the same assholes who hadn't done shit the whole thirteen years I'd known her. Well Tameka didn't know where Donna had moved to either, or at least that's what she told me, anyway. I didn't care about her moving. I just don't like not knowing where my enemies are when they know so much about me. One of my plans for the year was to restart my divorce from Donna and to ask Mica to move away with me and my baby. I knew I would need to get my money up quick, so I called up my old plug to bust one last power move. If it wasn't for finding out who was behind all the bullshit that had been happening to me, I wouldn't have made that call. But I needed to get away from it all, real far, and fast-like if I wanted to be happy.

Chapter 9

Why Won't You Stop

WHEN I HAVE A lot on my mind, my thoughts tend to race, and I need to do something, anything, with myself until I can calm down or the spell passes. I used to be embarrassed, well, more ashamed to admit that I suffer from manic depression. But I live and function well with it and even better when I'm taking my meds. Because this part of me was so hard to share once I broke up with Donna, I no longer had anyone that I trusted to make sure I was taking my meds properly. I thought I had a good thing going on my own when it came to taking my meds. First, I would try to work through the spells without them by working out or working on my cars. When that didn't work I would lock myself in my room for a few days and take the meds until I felt better. It wasn't until much later that I found out that Donna had been using my meds to control me. I'll get to that later in the story.

So I was in my room working through one of my spells that was brought on by the verification that Deidra was behind everything that had been going on with me. I'd just finished my sixth set of

fifty pushups, when the standard ringtone began playing on my cell. The tone told me that it was an unknown number. I usually wouldn't answer unknown numbers on this line, but since I'd called my old connect, I took a chance on it being him, and it was.

"What it do, stranger! I thought you had forgotten about your boy."

"Never that, my nig. I've just been going through it lately with these crazy bitches," I admitted, taking a set on my bed and staring at my reflection in the mirror in front of me that I'd taken off of the wall for no reason at all.

"Damn, fam, you still going through that shit with your seed and that lame-ass nigga?"

"Yeah, kinda. It's that shit and some other BS with these lames out here." I'd gotten close to my plug over the few years that we'd known each other. Mostly because we did time together in the Feds and I knew him to be a pretty stand-up dude.

"Well tell me something good. I know you ain't call me for the hell of it. Is we back on or what? Because I only got a book and a half left until the end of the month."

"Man, it's been real fucked up for me lately, like I said. I'm trying to bust a move with you, but I ain't got that kinda cash to work with right now," I told him honestly.

"Fam, miss me with that shit. I know you good for whatever, just give me what you working with and hit me with the rest on the bounce. I ain't tripping as long as you can get back by the end of the month when I go to the store."

"I can do that. Thanks, my nigga."

"Don't thank me, pay me." We laughed at the saying because it was a long-time running joke from how we got close in the Feds. But that's also another story for another time.

"So will you be ready in the morning?" I asked as I emptied the cash I had out of my king-size bed to count while watching a Hood 2 Hood DVD as we talked.

"Hell, I gotta come up there tonight to spend time with my lil bitch. You know how they get when they get knocked up an' shit." He chuckled. "But I can hit you when I touch and save you the trip."

"Sounds good to me. Just hit me when you're here. I got like ten waiting for you just so you know."

"That there is right on time. I gotta give my bitch like half of that for bills and to get the baby stuff," he admitted.

After a few more words we ended the call. I had actually kinda felt better with my focus on something other than my drama with Deidra and her goons. I made my way to the shower after finishing up my workout and posting a photo on Facebook asking my female friends if anyone of them wanted to join me. Mica called talking shit about my post and to let me know that she was pulling up to her job and that she would call me when she got settled in.

I took the shower, redressed, and continued to pass time on my page while working on writing a new novel titled Vengeful Guidance, that I hadn't had time to work on in a few days. Becoming a published author was another one of my goals that I set for myself for the year. I was going to see my work in print even if I had to self-publish it. It wasn't that my stories weren't good enough for the publishers I'd reached out to in the past. They just wasn't talking right for me, and Donna didn't really support my dream when we were together. So I put it off and only really used my writing to work through my spells.

My phone had shaken me out of a hot sex scene I was in the midst of writing. The standard tone told me who it was. But it was a text from my plug telling me that he was in town. I looked at the time and saw that it was almost two o'clock in the morning. But I hit him back telling him that I would meet him in the hood around the corner from our guy's barber shop. Then I gathered up the things I needed, my money and my gun, put on my dark brown Timberland boots that matched my leather hooded Pelle coat, and hit the streets. I drove my van over to my mother's to switch into my plum-colored 1999 Buick Riviera that I'd given to her. She never really used it, so I did because my plug knew the car but not the van, plus it was better on the lightly snow-covered streets. I needed that just in case I needed to get somewhere fast.

Yeah, I did tell you that my plug was a stand-up guy, but I don't trust no nigga at that time of the morning from out state, especially from Chicago, in a drought. Plus, with all of the other mess going on, hell yeah, I was being extra careful. Believe it or not,

this was the first time since I started dealing with him that I took a gun with me. We were just that real with one another. Donna's little sister, Tee, called me back finally. We talked on the phone as I drove to meet up with him. I wasn't in a rush because I knew that he wasn't there yet. I stopped at the twenty-four-hour gas station on Twenty-Seventh and Capital to get me a cranberry juice and some snacks for when I got the work from my guy and went home to put it together to be turned into the cash I needed. Plus I really just wanted the black plastic bag they gave out so I could put the cash in and keep my last cloth Crown Royal bag. They're hard to come by if you don't drink the stuff.

While sitting in the car at the gas pump, my guy called and said he was there waiting on me. I told him that I was right up the street and would be there in a hot second. Just as I was pulling away from the pumps, I saw Deidra pulling onto the lot. I knew it wasn't the right time to try to holla at her and let her know that I knew it was her fucking with me and to tell her to leave me the fuck alone. So I kept it moving. I really needed to get that work so a nigga could be outty on them bums.

As soon as I rounded the corner on Twenty-Fifth Street I spotted his flashy rose-gold Infiniti EX35 and parked behind it. I put my gun in my coat pocket, grabbed the bag of cash, and got out.

"I see you riding pretty." I looked around the interior of the truck once I got in with him. "I know you better not ever tell me that I need to be more lowkey when you're out here making moves in this bitch." At the same time as I was checking the truck out, I was checking our surroundings. That's when I spotted Deidra driving down the block.

"You're right, my nig, but I wasn't coming up here for this, remember? Anyways, I left the work at my bitch's crib when I got here. It's not that I don't trust you or no shit like that. I just seen plenty of police out here tonight around this muthafucka."

"It's cool. Here, it's ninety-five. I should have close to thirteen racks or more for you by the time you get ready to bounce later," I told him, handing him the cash.

"Fo sho, but I'ma be here about a week with her. Do you think you'll be done by then?"

"Yeah, hell yeah. You know how I do," I assured him. I looked around again to see if she was still around, then told him that I wanted to meet him in Wendy's parking lot before we parted ways. I knew he would take his sweet time as always and call me when he was ready, so I wasn't in a rush to get there either. There were a lot of police out that early morning hour and I didn't wanna be driving around with the gun on me, so I called Tiffany. She lived in the area and had been waiting on me to come by. On second thought, I didn't wanna lead her on or argue with her in case she felt some kinda way about the way I stopped messing with her. With that thought I decided to take my chances in the hood by riding around the area. I was just cruising down capital when I saw my cousin Queet, walking up the street. I pulled up on her to see where she was going at that hour. She said she was heading to the gas station to get cigarettes, blunts, and some more stuff. I dropped her back off at home and told her that I would bring it to her when I was done with my guy since I was gonna be up them ways. On my way back up Capital, I passed Deidra heading the other direction. I wanted to let her know that I'd seen her but just continued on to the station to get my cousin's order and wait there since it was across from Wendy's. When I walked out of the station, Deidra was sitting in the lot watching me. I got back in my car and saw that she was on the phone. I thought she might've been calling her goons, so I quickly pulled off and sped down Capital. She pulled off right behind me. I stomped on the gas, made a few quick turns, and then dipped into an alley and shut off my headlights so she wouldn't see where I'd gone.

I saw her storm past the alley where I was parked, so I gave her a few minutes before I drove out. I started to turn left but then made a right just in case she made a U-turn on me. I should've followed my first mind because I ran right into her at the corner. It was a stop sign, so I sat there allowing her to go her way so I could go mine, but she didn't move. So I slowly drove across the intersection, never breaking eye contact with her as I went. Once I crossed, Deidra moved forward and then stopped in the middle of the crossing, with her window now down.

I stopped in my tracks, threw the car in park, and got out holding my arms out to my sides, like, "What, I'm here, bitch. Come get some." I was pissed. She waved something at me, but I couldn't make out what it was because I was in the middle of the block. I gave her the finger and got back in the car. As I pulled off I noticed that she was still sitting there watching me. So now I was like, "Fuck this shit. This bitch must think I'm scared of her ass or something." I pulled over, parked, and then hopped right out and walked back toward her.

Deidra watched me approaching her on foot, drove up, and pulled over. I guessed she was waiting on me, but I didn't trust her like that to be walking in the street, so I got on the sidewalk in case she decided to try and run me over. Even though it was lightly, snowing and cold out, I didn't put my hood up to cover my big bald-ass head. I walked right around the front of her car to the driver's-side window. As soon as I got there, she got to popping slick at the mouth.

"What, bitch ass nigga! This here ain't what you want!" she said, and a lot more shit that I wasn't trying to hear.

"Bitch, fuck you! I ain't trying to argue with you. You can do that with your bitch! I just want you to leave me the fuck alone. I ain't fucking with y'all, so stop fucking with me. That's it, that's all I gotta say about this bullshit you on. Stop!" I told her through her slightly open window.

"Hoe ass nigga, get the fuck outta –" Her voice faded as she leaned over, reaching down with her right hand and then quickly coming back up with something shiny and dark from between the seat.

"Oh shit!" I yelled quickly, simultaneously pulling my gun from my pocket. I fired as I got out of her firing range. I wasn't really aiming, I was just trying to get the hell out of the way. I just ran once I had backed far enough away. I didn't stick around to find out if she had gotten hit, or for her to shoot at me. If she was gonna shoot me it was gonna be in the back as I ran away. Hell, the only reason I stopped running was because I slipped and fell when I cut through someone's yard. The fall hurt my knee, but that didn't stop me from making it back to my car.

I got in and pulled off but had to pull over and park again a few blocks away to get my nerves together. Now being in situations where I had to shoot my way out wasn't new to me. I grew up in the street, and I've banged it out with the best of 'em, but I've never had to go there with a female. It's rules to this street shit, believe it or not. No women or children is the one that had my head fucked up at the time. Once I felt okay enough to drive again, I did, and my mind automatically went into survival mode.

One of the first things I did was toss the gun after I toweled it down. Then I got back in the van and went over to Mica's. She was still at work, but

Sparkle was there to let me in because I'd forgotten my key at my place on my other keyring. I went straight into the bedroom to be alone so I could think. I noticed that I'd lost one of my phones, and, would you believe, it was the one I needed to get in touch with my plug. That saying is so true, "When it rains, it pours." I turned on the TV to try to find out some info about it on the news. I didn't see anything, so I didn't think she had been killed or nothing.

WHEN IS FAR ENOUGH?

Intent to kill means that one had the mental purpose to take the life of another or was aware that one's conduct was practically certain to cause the death of another.

Chapter 10

Detective's Interview

IN THE OFFICE THE atmosphere was pretty mello. I got a fresh cup of coffee and the number of this sexy beat cop that I'd had my eye on since she started. Just when I thought I was going to have an easy shift, we got called to a possible homicide. I really didn't feel like dealing with this shit right now. But I knew the first forty-eight hours of a homicide gave us the best chances of catching the scumbag that pulled the trigger. I pulled up to the scene and scoped out the environment. I saw people standing around crying and screaming. It' always helpful to have a close family member or friend to help start things off, and right now we had the sister of the vic as our first witness interview.

"Please, ma'am, Let's get in my squad car, get out of this cold, and talk." She agreed, and once we got inside the car, I turned up the heat. "I know this is hard for you right now, but anything you can think of might help us catch the person who did this."

"Yeah, yeah, okay." She dried her tears with her hands then took another look up the street at the scene.

"Please state your full name for me, please?" I asked with my pen and pad ready. "Lashann Herling."

"Okay, Lashann, I'm Detective Hooker, and the guy that pointed you my way is my partner, McKnight. Ma'am, whenever you're ready, tell me when was the last time that you saw the vic—I'm sorry, your sister?"

She took a moment to clear her tears again before she began.

"Oh God, please give me the strength, give me the strength!" she prayed in a whisper. "We was at our nightclub together just hanging out. Deidra had worked the night with me from 9:00 p.m. to close."

"And what time was that?"

"Around 1:45. We actually closed the club together. She should have had a large amount of

money on her from the night's sales at the club."
She looked away from me back toward the scene.
"We walked out together, got in our cars, and went
our separate ways."

"Did she tell you where she was going?"

"No, she never said."

"Can you think of anyone that she might have met
up with?"

"Deidra got two girlfriends that I can think of here,
and her wife lives out of state. I know one of her
girlfriends live over on Keefe somewhere. I can't
think of her name. The other one's name is Donna,
and the last place I knew she stayed was a few
houses from the club."

"Can you describe this Donna for me? Just do
your best. Like I said, anything would help me get
to the bottom of this."

"Okay. Let me see. She's about five foot nine,
160 pounds, dark skin with dark slanted eyes, and
I guess medium-length hair."

I wrote down the description, and she went on to
tell me that she believed they dated for approx.-
imately five months. She then related to me an
incident that took place between Deidra and
Donna.

"Do you know when their relationship started?"

"Around the summer of 2011," she answered, then went on to explain that at this time the husband of the girlfriend had pistol-whipped Donna for about two days in an attempt to identify the subject she was having relations with. Lashann said Donna related back to Deidra that she never revealed her identity.

"About how long ago did this happen?"

"Ooooh, I say about two months ago."

Now two months ago wasn't the summer, so something didn't fit. That alone was enough for me to have a talk with this Donna. Now anyone who could take a beating like the one Lashann described, I had to meet.

"Where were you when your sister was shot?"

"I was at Potawatomi Bingo, gambling. That's why she had all of the money on her." This was the second time she said something about money. I made a note to run a background check on both of them as soon as we were done here. "I got a call from Bill, our security guy at the club, saying that Ralonda had just called him saying that Deidra got shot."

"Who is Ralonda to Deidra?"

"She's her girlfriend."

"Do you know how I can get in touch with her?" I took down the info Ms. Herling had on Ralonda. Then she went on to tell me that she remembered her sister telling her that Donna lived in the neighborhood of the shooting.

"I called my brother to go around the corner to check for Deidra because he lives in this area. I got mad at him for asking too many questions and hung up on him. I really started panicking when our mother started calling. After telling my mother, I would call her as soon as I found her, I started calling around and drove to the nearest hospital, but she wasn't there. So I headed to the county hospital to see if she was there. That's when my mother called and told me that it was true, Deidra did get shot and was on the way to the county hospital. I was the first one there, so I waited for the rest of the family to get there. After the hospital told me that I could not see her, I decided to go to where she got shot. I found it when I seen her car," she said, looking back at the scene once again.

"Can you tell me more about –" I looked back over my notes until I found the name. "About Donna?"

Lashann took a deep breath and then stated that she could positively identify Donna. She said she had seen her dozens of times before in their club and that Donna was in fact there on New Year's Eve. I asked her if she knew what type of car Donna drove?

"A Dodge Durango? Yeah, it's a white Durango. Donna is kinda jealous of Ralonda but knew her position and about Ralonda in the beginning of the relationship. Deidra is a big weed smoker, but she don't sell drugs."

"Okay, Ms. Herling, that's all for now, but I may contact you about the identity of Donna if need be."

"That's fine. I'ma help anyway I can."

I thanked her and concluded my interview with the sister of the vic. The more I thought about this case, the more I was guessing it was something between a bad drug deal or a lovers' spat turned deadly. Hopefully I'd have a better take on things after I compared notes with McKnight, who at this time seemed to have his hands full talking with the two black males that flagged the officer down to alert them to the car with the gunshot victim inside. I could see now that I didn't want any part of the mess he was dealing with over there. I'd just run the names that Ms. Herling provided me with and see what came up.

Chapter 11

Painful Curiosity

MY THOUGHTS WERE RACING so fast that they had me paralyzed in the spot I was sitting in bed. I don't know how much time had passed from the shooting to the time I'd made it to the house. I guessed I was in shock or something because things shouldn't have gone the way they had. After awhile I snapped out of the daze and turned on the news again. I kept flipping between two channels, 58 and 12, because my godmother had always told me that if I needed to know what was going on in the hood, I could always count on those channels to report it.

That night they seemed to be useless. I couldn't

find any station talking about the shooting. No, I wasn't gloating about what happened. I really wanted to know if I had killed her so I could think. If Deidra was alive, I had a better chance in court once she told on me. I didn't know if she was cut like that or not, but I did know that the police were always called when it was a shooting. If she was a man, I wouldn't have been so worried, because most niggas that play the streets keep it in the streets. That's what I know and what I'm used to. Just because she dressed like a man and did her best to emulate one, at the end of the day Deidra was still a woman, and the courts were only going to see that part of her. I would've just beat her ass if she wanted to fight and not pulled that gun.

I continued flipping through the channels, but the TV still wasn't hitting on shit, so I tried my luck on Facebook. It was there that I first heard about the shooting, but I was getting so many mixed reports, I didn't know what to believe. Some people posted that she had died, and others said she was at the hospital on life support. It was all too much and had my head pounding. So I lay down and tried to sleep it off, but couldn't. I needed to get up with my plug so I could get my money back or the work, so I could put some real cash in a lawyer's hand first just in case I needed one. I tossed and turned in bed until Mica walked in from work. I wanted to tell her so bad what had happened, but just couldn't. I pulled her onto the bed with me and held her.

"What's wrong, bae?" she asked, wiggling out of my embrace. The less she knew, the better for her. I pulled her back and kissed her before I answered her.

"Nothing, I just need you in my arms right now."

"Noo, bae, let me wash them people off me first. I smell like work." She pulled away from me again, this time smiling as she began undressing for her shower. Any other time watching her sexy self getting undressed would've put me there with her. I would've been tossing her short ass around until we exploded and passed out together. But I felt nothing that night. I allowed her to go take her shower while I checked back in on Facebook to see if anything solid had been posted about Deidra.

Sometime later Mica just materialized in front of me wrapped in towels.

"Bae, I think I need to go to the hospital."

"Why, what's wrong?" I asked, putting down my phone.

"I'm spotting and I got a sharp pain in my stomach. I thought I could deal with it at first, but now it's worse," she explained with tears running down her face.

"Okay–" I could see that she was in pain. "Get dressed. How long have you been like this?" I asked, putting on my things.

"I don't know, maybe almost a month."

"Why in the fuck would you wait so long?"

"Don't yell bae."

"I'm sorry. But you should've said something way sooner." I shook my head and listened as she dressed so we could go.

Once we were at the hospital I had my brother, Ty, meet me there. I put him up on as much of what was going on as I could. I was trusting him to come through for me with the lawyer and or bail money if I needed it. Everything about that day felt wrong. Something deep inside of me told me that Deidra was gone, that I'd taken her life, but before I could get back on the subject I needed to make sure Mica was alright. When she was done with all of the checkups, all she told me was that they had given her something for the pain and told her to follow up with her doctor.

I didn't think much of it because of the big issue

that I was dealing with. But on the drive back to her house I could tell some more was on her mind that she wasn't telling me. I wondered if she'd seen something on Facebook about what had happened and didn't know how to ask me about it. Then again, I knew that couldn't be it because I had never told her anything about it. She didn't need to know about the bullshit between me and Deidra.

I got her home, in bed, and fed. I was just holding her and wondering what was going on, what my next move was. That's when my phone rang letting me know I had a text from Apple. She was my uncle's stepdaughter and a friend with benefits. I don't know how to label our relationship. I don't even remember how we started messing around, for real. But she needed me to fix her car, and I needed to do something with myself because I was worrying myself to death thinking about Deidra's well-being. I texted her back and told her that I was on my way.

"Hey, Mica, will you be alright for a bit? I gotta go help Apple with her car right quick."

"Yeah, I'ma go to sleep. Can you bring me some orange juice back?"

"Okay, is that all?"

She said yeah, and I walked to the store with her oldest son. We also stopped at Micky D's on Wisconsin, on our way back so I could get him something to eat since his mother was down for the count. After I got him back home and gave Mica her juice, I got in my van and shot down to Apple's place.

"I'm outside by your car," I told her once she answered my call.

"Okay, mister, I'm finna put on my boots and be right out since you wanna act like you can't come in."

"It's not like that. It just don't make sense to come in when I'm already out here," I explained, trying to chill her attitude. "Why you leave your keys in the car?" I asked, noticing them when I looked through her car window.

"That's what's wrong with the car. The key stuck," she answered, coming outside the house.

I looked up and saw her walking toward me and hung up on her. Then I tried the car door and found it wasn't locked. I shook my head as I sat in the driver's seat to try to figure out the issue with the ignition switch. The first thing I noticed was that the gearshift wasn't in park. I gave it a push, and just like that, it released the key.

"Girl!"

"What? How you do that so fast?" I handed her the key. "What did you do, so I'll know next time?"

"Your drunk ass didn't have the car in park. Let me find out you was just trying to get me over here," I joked, because I hadn't been spending much time with her lately.

"For your info, I wasn't drinking last night, and if I wanted your ass to come over here, you would've been over here." She snapped her fingers and then said, "I don't know how I forgot that." She laughed at herself.

"Well, if you wasn't drunk, then you were high as a muthafucka and couldn't pay attention to what you were doing. I told you about that shit. Don't make me put you on no smoke for a week."

"Baby, don't do me like that." She hugged me. "Is you coming in, or do you gotta run?"

"No, I can stay for a minute." I followed her into the house.

"Assa, did you hear about that gay girl that got shot in her car last night?" Apple, asked retrieving her unfinished blunt from the ashtray and relighting it.

"That gay girl?" I pulled her down so she was sitting on my leg to make it easier to talk to her without her moving around.

"The one that owns that bar by your old bitch crib."

"Do you know if she died or not?"

"Nope. Muthafuckas saying all typa shit on Facebook about her. I don't know what to believe." She took a pull off the blunt and blew it out away from me.

"I did that dumbass shit," I blurted out. I don't know why I told her, but I did. I knew I needed someone to talk to that I could trust not to repeat anything.

"What do you mean you did that?" She stood up looking me right in my eyes, I guessed to see if I was being serious with her.

"Man, ma, I was trying to bust this move, and ol' girl got to following me an' shit. So I pulled over to talk to her, and then she got to talking crazy and up'd on me, so I shot and got the fuck outta the way," I explained as clear and honest as I could.

"Assa, why would she be following you? Didn't the bitch know better than to be fucking with you?" Apple thought for a second, then added, "Oh shit, she's the one Donna , your ex-wife, is fucking with, ain't she?"

"Yep. And she the one that's been behind all that bullshit that's been going on with me and my guys getting robbed." I stood up and started pacing. I needed to be doing something when I was worried, and pacing sometimes helped.

"Did you kill her?" she asked, taking hold of my hand to stop me.

"Hell, I don't know. I just started shooting and moving so I didn't get shot back. I've been looking at the news channels all morning trying to find out what's going on with her."

"I don't know how you ain't seen it, because it's been on all of the channels since I turned on the TV."

"I don't know. It must have came on while I was at the hospital with Mica. Did they say how she was doing?"

"I don't think so. Baby, what we gonna do?"

"Shit, I don't know yet. I lost my other phone last night when I fell, and I need it so I can get the work I was waiting to get when it happened. So I can get ready for whatever happens next."

"I don't think she finna tell the police shit because

she be on that setting-niggas-up shit, and I know she sells weed too. But you go where your guy at and get your stuff or money back."

"Yeah, that's what I gotta do when I leave here." I broke away from her and started pacing around the kitchen again.

That's when Dream called and told me that Deidra was dead. Then she turned right around in the same breath and said that she wasn't. So I was still confused. Dream asked me to come over and talk to her. I agreed because I knew she knew more than she was letting on. Dream had a strong connection with the LGBT community, so she heard things, plus she knew about the relationship between my ex and Deidra. There was not too much she didn't know about me.

"Hey, I'll be back over here later. I'm finna go see what Dream gotta say. Hey, Apple, do this for me? Go on your page and see if you can find out what hospital ol' girl in or whatever else you can find out."

She agreed and I headed over to Dream's. On the drive over I thought about my baby and what would happen to her if I got locked up. I knew Dream could help me with her while I was out there, but I wasn't sure if she was cut like that to keep dealing with her until I got things straight with all of this mess. I was thinking about the charges I might have to fight. Reckless use of a dangerous weapon, reckless homicide, or maybe negligence. All of them would take me away from my family for years. I just needed to know her fate so I could try and judge mines.

Chapter 12

Second Detective Interview

TIME WAS TICKING WITH this shooting, and we were still trying to get going.

"Let's stop for food before we head in," McKnight suggested while finishing up his notes of leads we had to follow up on.

"Sounds like a plan to me. I can always eat."

I headed toward Jimmy John's.

"Hey, that woman you interviewed this morning, didn't you say that she was the girlfriend of the vic?"

"Yeah, I believe her name is Ralonda, why?"

"Well, I spoke with the sister, and she said that the vic had at least three women that she was dealing with at the same time. I'm thinking we should pay this Donna a visit. I ran backgrounds on the names the sister gave me, and this Donna and her husband are two of them that we most certainly need to have a conversation with."

"Okay, but I need food right afterward, or I'm going to pass out," he said, and I turned the car around. I wanted to hearhat she could tell us about our vic's drug sales. I found out that not only was she a heavy smoker, but she sold weed as well, from the girlfriend I spoke with."

"Oh really? Run your interview with her back by me right quick. The officers that escorted the ambulance to the hospital reported that the vic had a large amount of both cocaine and marijuana on her person. But the sister made it her business to stress to me that the vic did not sell drugs and that the money found on her was from the drink sales at their nightclub," I explained as I pulled over across from Donna's address. I parked and let my partner recap his interview.

"Ms. Ralonda Randal stated at approximately 3:50 a.m. that she had just come from the hospital, after being advised that Deidra had died. She stated that she brought in the New Year with Deidra at their family-owned nightclub and they were there until 7:00 a.m. on 01/01/12. Ralonda stated to her knowledge the vic had not had any problems with anyone at the club that night. After celebrating they returned to Ralonda's residence, where they slept until the early afternoon."

"They slept, huh? I would've loved to be a fly on the wall watching them sleep," I joked.

"Hey, you and me, both, but don't interrupt me again, or you'll be reading this shit yourself."

"Okay, okay, carry on." I gulped down the last of my cold coffee.

"Let me see here. Where was I?. .. Okay. The vic left Ralonda's home around 7:00 p.m. saying she was going to go get the club ready to open for business. She said the next time she spoke with Deidra was around 1:00 a.m. when she called her on her cell phone. The vic answered at that time and told her that she was just leaving the club and was heading home. During this conversation, Ralonda indicated she could hear Deidra talking to someone who Deidra said was her sister, Lashann, who also works at the club. After walking her sister to the car, Deidra focused her attention on the phone call between her and Ralonda. They talked for the next twenty minutes as the vic drove home. At one point Ralonda asked Deidra if she was home yet because she knew it didn't take that long for her to drive home from the club. Deidra responded that she was at home, and they continued their conversation, discussing their plans for later that day. A short time later she said she heard rumbling as if Deidra had dropped the phone. The phone line remained open for the next ten minutes as Ralonda kept yelling the vic's name but got no response. Ralonda stated that she didn't hear any gunshots or other voices just prior to or after she heard Deidra's scream."

"What scream? You didn't say anything about a scream."

"Look, I'm trying to bring you up to speed on this the best I can on an empty belly. So maybe I said it or maybe I didn't, but it was a scream. Now let me finish."

"Hey, I'm just trying to get the facts straight, man."

"Ralonda said she could hear unknown male voices on the open line saying something to the effect of, 'She's not breathing. She's shot.' She states that she panicked and hung up the phone and then immediately called back but didn't get an answer. She repeatedly called the phone to no avail."

"Okay, hold up right there a moment. Is there any mention about drugs or money in your interview with her? If so, just skip right to that."

"Yes, in fact there was. Ms. Ralonda stated that the vic had been selling marijuana since they've been together. On occasions Deidra would take her along when she would make transactions, and to her knowledge the vic would initiate a transaction after receiving a call from a buyer."

"Did she know of any of the vic's buyers who live in this area?"

"Not that she knew of. Ralonda can only speculate that the vic may have been trying to serve someone from a call. She did indicate that she doesn't know who would want to hurt Deidra and that Deidra wasn't seeing anyone else intimately."

"Well that's funny. I bet Ms. Jones wouldn't see it that way from what Ms. Herling told me." Right now I'm not sure what to make of this case. All I know is that I really need to have a talk with this Donna Jones to put more of the puzzle together. "Okay, old buddy, let's get this over with so I can feed you, because you're not yourself when you're hungry."

"Ha-ha, Mr. Funny. Let's go." McKnight got out of the squad car first. "Which one is it?" he asked once

I followed suit.

"The house right in front of us." McKnight rang the doorbell, and it was answered right away by a cute little black girl approximately ten years old. After he told her who we were and that we would like to speak with her mother, the little girl ran off and brought back her mother. The woman fit the description of Donna Jones that was given to me by the vic's sister.

"Ms. Jones, we would like to talk to you about the shooting that took place up the street from here earlier this morning. Do you mind if we come in for a second, or would you like to talk in the car?" I asked.

"No, you can come in." She turned to who I speculated were her children. "Hey, y'all go in your rooms so I can talk with them in peace!" Donna ordered them as she led us into her living room to talk. I took a seat on the sofa, and McKnight stood next to it.

"Is your husband here? We would like to speak with him as well," I said, looking around the place.

"No, we're separated. What do he got to do with anything?"

"Maybe nothing. We are just dotting our I's and

crossing our T's, that's all," McKnight explained.

"Can you tell me why you two separated?" I asked, pulling out my notepad.

"We broke up after a domestic battery incident." She looked a little nervous as she answered.

"When was the last time you spoke with him?" She took out her phone and reviewed her call log.

"Last month on the 28th."

"Can I see that please?" McKnight asked, taking the phone from her hands to observe the display on the screen. He wrote down the number and then gave it back to her.

"I didn't talk to him when he called, so he texted me this." She pulled up the text message and handed the phone back to him.

McKnight read it to himself first and then out loud to me: "This is bye for real. It's not what I wanted for us, but it is what it is. I miss my babies, and I'm scared, but I'm just holding on to a family I fucked off. I'ma keep my end up on the van. Please let me talk to my baby B4 I go." He wrote down the text before he handed the phone back again.

"Does he own a gun that you know of?" I asked.

"Yeah, I seen him with two, a .40 caliber and a 9 mm handgun. He always has one of them with him, on his person or in his car."

"What's your relationship with Deidra Herling?"

"We are dating, why?"

"Did you ever hear him make threats to hurt Ms. Herling?"

"No. He never said anything about her. When he found out about us, the only thing he did was threaten to kill hisself over our breakup, but I never heard him say anything bad about Deidra."

"Has he come by your house at all since then?" McKnight asked.

"No. He don't know where I moved to."

"Do you know his shoe size?"

"Yeah, he wears a ten and a half or eleven. Why? Do y'all think he had something to do with her death?" She looked back and forth from my face to McKnight's waiting for an answer.

"We're just doing our job and following all leads. Tell me, how do you know about the shooting?"

"I found out from her sister, Lashann. She called me earlier, and that's when I realized the shots I heard last night might've been her."

"And what were you doing when you heard these shots?"

"I was looking at TV with my kids in my bedroom. I didn't pay the shooting no mind because I hear them in this neighborhood all the time. I think it was about one when I heard the shots. Then maybe a half hour later I seen police lights in front of my house, but I didn't think it had anything to do with Deidra."

McKnight sat down beside me on the sofa. "How long have you and Herling been dating?" he asked, taking the question right out of my mouth.

"About two years. Deidra has another girl she's involved with named Ralonda. I think they were together for like eight years, from what she told me."

We asked Donna a few more questions to get a better understanding of her relation to the vic, then ended the interview and left. I allowed McKnight to drive while I compared my notes with his, plus I didn't want him running me around as he tried to make up his mind on where to eat. I made a note to talk to the sister again and to find out if there was any truth to what Donna told us about an unknown female making threats to the vic and saying that she had AIDS. If the AIDS thing was true, then maybe this female was our killer.

After a short phone call, McKnight made a U-turn

and headed east.

"I guess we eating Burger King. That was just the other girlfriend asking me to come talk to her there."

"I hope she has something good to tell us because I really don't have a taste for the King today." I went back to writing my notes. I thought of what was said in Donna's interview and told him that I wanted to go have a talk with the sister again after we were finished with Ralonda. This was turning out to be a long day. I shook my head trying to shake the first of; I'm sure, many migraines. "Hey, let's blow through a few of these lights so we can get this over with. I need a nap."

"I was just about to hit the siren." He turned on the siren and the lights and then did about 50 mph through traffic.

Ms. Ralonda was waiting for us outside smoking a cigarette. McKnight pulled into the open parking spot right in front of her, and she walked over and got in the backseat of the car. As soon as the door closed, she told us that their vic had an affair with a female named Donna. I pulled out the photo of the woman I believed she was talking about, and she confirmed that the photo of Ms. Jones was indeed the Donna she was talking about. Ralonda told us that on two separate occasions she had confrontations with Donna. She said it wasn't until today she learned that Donna lived just up the street from where Deidra was killed. She said she put two and two together and thought that maybe Donna and her husband had something to do with her death. We took down notes of every word she said before letting her out of the squad car. I asked her to sign the photo I showed her of Ms. Jones, just in case I needed her to pick her out in a line-up. Then we grabbed something to eat, on her, through the drive-thru and were on our way to take a short break for the day.

"Didn't you say that you didn't want the King today?"

"Yeah, but free is always good," I answered, then stuffed a few french fries in my mouth.

Chapter 13

A Maze of Dead Ends

WHEN I MADE IT over to Dream's, I saw that two of her sisters were there with here. It really wasn't unusual for them to be there, because they're a very close family, but I got a feeling when I entered the room with them that made me pay attention to their every movement. Dream did all the talking to me, which again wasn't unusual, because me and her mostly talked about the kids or things that needed to be done around her crib. What was unusual was that they were hanging on my every word. I told them I didn't know about the shooting. I didn't want to lie to them, especially to Dream, but the less they knew, the better for them and me once the truth came out. Well, from them I learned that

Deidra had died for sure. My heart broke a little because I just knew things were going to go way down from there. I told Dream that I loved her, so she would be sure to know how much our friendship meant to me. It still means a lot even though we don't talk as much as I would like to.

Anyway, I had called my baby and taken her into her bedroom and told her that I had messed up bad and that I might be going to jail. I told her that so she could get in touch with my mother when it happened and told her that she should mind Dream until I got things together. When I left Dream's house I went looking for my guy so I could get the money or the work from him.

~ ~ ~

"You just missed him. He left about an hour ago," the soon-to-be mother informed me as I stood talking with her on the porch of her crib.

"Shit! Fuck! Did he say when he was coming back?"

"He told me that he was staying until you had the baby."

"Yeah, he was, but he said that some nigga that he came up here to meet with might have shot that chick the other night."

"Why would he think that?"

"I don't know. All I know is he said he didn't want to be around if the nigga tried to use him as a get-out-of-jail-free card. I hope he don't get caught up in somebody else bullshit."

"Don't worry, he won't." I pulled out a piece of paper that I'd written my number down on before I got out of the van, and handed it to her. "Here, call him and tell him to get up with me ASAP. I just lost my other phone. This my new number. And tell him that things are swell on my end. I'm just waiting on him. She told me she would tell him and I believed her. I got back in the van disappointed, but understood where he was coming from. I would've done the same thing until I found out more of what was going on with him. As soon as I pulled away from her I received a call from Tameka asking if I could come pick her up from on the south side where I had dropped her off at. I had to head that way, and I was just passing time waiting on my guy to call, so I told her I'd do it. When I got there she and my nephew were waiting outside for me.

"Sis, you look mad. What happened?" I asked once they were in the van.

"Nothing. That bitch in there just got to tripping the fuck out a few minutes ago, and I had to bust him in his shit. I don't wanna talk about it. Do you got something to smoke? I need to calm my nerves."

"Nope, but it seems like we're both having bad days." I didn't know why I felt the need to tell her about things, but I did. She had always been there for me when I needed someone to talk to. I told her pretty much what went down, but not all of it. "Hey, if I don't get to see you again, just know I love you, sis!"

"Boy, don't talk like that. Things gonna work out. I love you too! That bitch was fucking with you, and you just did what you had to to save yourself." She got quiet for a moment, then said, "You need to get up with your guy so you can get things together. Don't get to tripping and give up; just take a few and think. You need to make sure you're good."

I agreed then dropped them off at her friend's. I decided to make my way over to my mother's house just because. I didn't tell her what I had done, just that I had messed up bad and it wasn't looking good for me at the moment. I also did the same with my uncles. I was just saying goodbye to the ones I loved. I did get up with a few niggas that owed me money and collected what I could. My mind was really fucked up now that I knew for sure that she was dead.

I got the call from Donna's other sister, Neek. She needed my help with her truck. My heart broke a little more because I knew I had a lot of people that depended on me a lot. I couldn't help her myself, so I called my guy Chris to give her a hand, but still went over and waited with her until he got out there. While waiting I talked to her to try to find out as much as I could about what she knew about what went down. Neek told me that the police had talked to Donna asking her about me, but she didn't tell them much of anything. She said that Donna told them that I couldn't have had anything to do with it because I didn't know where she lived and that Deidra would've called her if she had seen me anywhere in the area. That news put me at ease some, but I didn't trust it completely because why would they be looking for me? I had thought that maybe Deidra had told them my name before she died. I said fuck it and went back to Mica's knowing I needed to get off the streets since I wasn't really doing anything at the time. Plus I needed to tell her what was going on so she could prepare herself for whatever came next. Then I had a second thought that I'd better wait until I put some money in the lawyer's hand and tell her how to get in touch with him just in case them people got ahold of me before I was ready for them to.

I knew if I turned myself in with a lawyer, it would look better on me and I may get a break or a real chance at telling my side of the story. So far the story that was being put together by people on Facebook wasn't sounding too good. I never meant to kill her or to even really hurt her; it was just my reflexes from growing up in the ghetto.

I made it back to Mica's and climbed in bed with her, holding her close. I had gotten upset with her because she was going in to work that night. She swore to me that she was feeling better and that she wouldn't have much work to do when she got there. So I left it alone and we just chilled until it was time for her to go in. I made sure to get a kiss and tell her that I loved her before she went in to work. I was just sitting there going over the info that was being posted on Facebook when I got a text from Apple asking me when was I coming back over. I had forgotten that I told her that I was coming back. I responded telling her that I was on my way. No, my mind wasn't on fucking her. I just didn't want to be alone, and I still had a really bad feeling that something was about to happen. It was the same feeling that I had when the shooting took place that

I'd ignored, so I didn't ignore it again.

On the way over I was thinking that I had to make sure that my baby was okay. I did honestly believe that she was in good hands where she was, but I was still worried about her. I wasn't as worried about my other daughter because her mother was always on top of her job as a mother. I just couldn't fucking believe that I was leaving them again.

Apple answered the door dressed in a sexy teddy and smoking a blunt. Right then I knew what she had on her mind, but mine wasn't there. I followed her phat butt up to her bedroom, but even watching the sway of her hips dressed the way she was didn't change my mood for sex. Apple knew things were weighing heavy on my mind. Even though I could see her disappointment, she still assured me that she would be there for me in any way she could be. So all we ended up doing was sitting in bed letting the TV watch us as we talked about what I could do.

I'ma be honest with y'all, for the first time in my life I seriously thought of taking a nice long deep hit off her blunt to try and ease my stress. But I knew it wouldn't help. I was wondering why in the fuck my plug hadn't called me back yet. Now if I would've gone back over to his bitch's crib and drug her ugly ass up and down the damn block, I bet his ass would've show up then. At this time I really didn't need to be alone because my thoughts were really, really confused.

Chapter 14

3rd Detective Interview

SLOUCHED IN MY CHAIR, I put my feet up on the desk in my cozy cubicle replaying the second interview I had with the vic's sister. Ms. Herling did admit to speaking with Donna Jones yesterday. She also told me that the conversation took place at her nightclub, Sisters. Ms. Herling indicated that Donna came there with an unknown female inquiring about what happened to the vic. During this conversation, Herling stated that she told Donna that she believed her husband had something to do with her sister's death. Donna told her that she did not believe her husband had anything to do with it because she hadn't been dealing with him for over a year.

Now none of these times fell into place for me. I really needed to have a sit-down with Mr. Jones so I could get his side of things. McKnight spoke with a friend of the victim, named Christol, who stated that Donna's sister, Neek, would tease Mr. Jones because his wife left him for a woman. When I asked Herling this, she said Christol provided her with some information related to her sister's death. She told her that a friend of hers knew Ray Jones, and according to that friend he was extremely upset about the relationship between Donna and the vic. Herling also said Christol told her that she had multiple talks with the victim about Ray and was concerned with her safety because of how upset he was.

As soon as McKnight got me the address of this friend where Mr. Jones was known to hang out, I planned to go have a talk with her and him. Hopefully we could catch him over there since no one seemed to have an address for him. I knew if what they said was true about the amount of teasing and taunting that Ray was going through with them, I would have snapped myself.

"Hooker, I have the address. I'll be ready to roll out in five minutes, if that's okay?" McKnight said suddenly, appearing and slapping a notepad on my desk.

"Yeah, okay, but let's make that more like twenty minutes. I just kicked my feet up." I chuckled, and he just shook his head before going to chase behind a hot little uniformed officer. I didn't know why he didn't just give up with her. That had to be some really good ass to have him working the way he was. Hell, that gal had way too much going on in the back, for my liking, but was sure good to look at from here.

~ ~ ~

I looked over at the clock in the dash and saw it was almost 11:00 p.m. when we pulled to a stop in front of the address of Dream Johassen. I allowed McKnight to take the lead on this one once I found out that Ray wasn't there. My partner began his line of questioning while I watched two little dogs play peek-a-boo with me from behind the sofa.

"Ms. Johassen, we're investigating the shooting death of Deidra Herling. A CI of ours pointed us here."

"I don't understand, why?" she interrupted.

"Do you know Ray Jones?"

"Yes, he's a good friend of mine, why? What do he got to do with this?"

"That's what we are here trying to find out," I told her, and then asked her how long she had known Mr. Jones, since my partner was beating around the bush.

"I've known him for some years. We dated awhile back but then decided to just be friends."

"We were told that you help take care of his daughter. Is that true?" McKnight asked.

"Yeah, I help him with her because after he received custody of her back in May of last year, his living arrangement was unstable, so I agreed to help him until he got things together," she explained.

"So you take care of his kid, and he does what exactly?" I asked, trying to get a better understanding of Ray.

"He's a good father. He do a lot for her. It's not like he just dropped her off on me. He pays some of the bills and for food and whatever for her. Assa is just trying to get back on his feet from the breakup with his wife."

"Okay, Ms. Johassen, how about you tell us about what you were doing the night of January first between the hours of, No, just start from around say ten, and I'll let you know when I have what I need," McKnight told her.

Johassen went on to state that on Sunday night she had talked to Mr. Jones on the phone twice. The last time was around 11:00 p.m., when he told her he would call her back. She stated she fell asleep, and then she got a call from Jones on the 2nd at 2:00 a.m., but they didn't talk because she told him she was sleeping.

"How are you so sure of the times?" McKnight asked.

"I got them right here in my call logs." She picked up her cell phone from the coffee table and showed it to us after she pulled up the calls. Then she went on to state that the next morning she received a call from her friend Christol telling her that Deidra had been killed. Johassen said that she called Jones and asked him if he knew anything about Deidra getting killed. She stated he asked her how he was supposed to know about that.

"How do you know the victim again, Ms. Johassen?"

She answered saying that she knew her from various nightclubs and bars. She stated that she knew that Ray's ex-wife, who was now gay, was dating Deidra. She also stated that Jones did come by her house around 1:00 p.m. and talk to her about various subjects. Then he called his daughter into her bedroom and talked to her for a few minutes and then left. She stated that this was odd for him to do because he had never done it before and that he may have put something in his daughter's room. So she had her sister come pick up the kids up so she could search the room.

"Do you mind if we have a look around here now?" I asked, thinking we might find something she missed in her search.

"Go right ahead. I don't got nothing to hide."

We went off to do a little friendly search. I had to stop McKnight from really tossing her place. Like I said, this was friendly, so there was no need to destroy her house. Plus the children were there, and I can't be mean to the kiddies.

Well we didn't find Mr. Jones hiding anywhere, nor did we find anything illegal. Johassen gave us Jones's phone numbers and the name of his Facebook page, and then we concluded our interview and left her home.

Chapter 15

How Did They Find Her?

"ASSA, WHERE YOU AT?" Dream asked as soon as I answered her call. I told her that I was in the city guessing that was what she was asking because I was always in and out of town. "The police just came to my house looking for you, asking me all types of questions about you and shit. What did you do?"

"What? Why did they come there?" Then I thought about it. "I'm on my way there," I told her, sliding from under Apple, who had fallen asleep on my lap.

"No, stay where you at. We not there. The kids over my mother's, and I'm on my way to get a drink. I'll call you when I get where I'm going, because we gotta talk."

"Okay, okay. Fuck!" I cursed more to myself than to her.

"Rayson, what's wrong?" Apple asked, waking up from me moving her.

"Hold on!" I retuned back to my call with Dream. I had a million questions for her, but she was too upset so I kept them to myself. "Hey, I'm finna just go into the police station and see what's up. I'll call you when I can or when I'm done there, so keep your phone on."

"Wait – Okay," Dream answered.

I knew she wanted to ask more questions, but I just couldn't answer them, so I ended the call before she could. As I put on my shoes, I hit the remote start on the van while repeating what Dream told me to Apple.

"Rayson, wait. I'm coming with you. I'll tell them you was with me that night, so they won't lock you up," she said, rushing to get herself dressed.

I thought about what she was suggesting. I knew it would give me some more time to get my shit together for the day when I was really ready to turn myself in for the shooting. Yeah, I had planned to turn myself in on it. I didn't mean to do it—well, want to do it, and it was really fucking with my head. I didn't know how they knew I knew Dream or why they didn't hit my mother's house first looking for me. That's been my home address on file forever. I should have asked her if it was the police or the Feds. Because the Feds would be the only ones that would go raid the homes of the people you least expected them to, looking for you.

"Okay, think about what you gonna say, and tell me when I get back, so I know."

"Nope, I'm coming with you right now, Rayson. I know you're just trying to keep me out of it," she told me, taking hold of my hand.

"No, I'm not. I want you to come with me just in case they keep me so you can tell Uncle Curt where I'm at and what's going on."

"Where you going then?"

"To get Mica's niece so she can tell them what time I got over there that night."

"Why, what for?"

"It'll help if I can show my whereabouts that night. I can't just say I was out riding around," I explained. Then she let me leave to go get Sparkle. I hoped that this plan of Apple's worked to buy me time. I really needed to make sure my kids were alright and that I had a lawyer so I wouldn't get so much time.

Well, if nothing else happened I knew I would have to do time for the gun if I gave it to them. I was kinda on the fence about that at the time. I wished I could have talked to my uncle about it, but I didn't have time. In my head my time was running out. I felt like they were watching my every move somehow. I told myself that I would get with everybody in the morning and tell them what was going on so they could help me through the mess I had gotten myself in.

~ ~ ~

I picked up Sparkle and met back up with Apple outside of her house. I got in the car with her so we could talk about things for a few minutes before getting back in the van and driving to the nearest police station. That ended up being the one on Fiftieth and

Lisbon. Apple followed us in her car so she could leave as soon as she was done talking to them.

Inside the station a female officer at the front desk told us to have a seat after I explained to her why I was there. She said she called the detective in charge of the case and he would be there in a few.

I wanted to leave right then. Everything in me told me to just go, but then it would look like I was running, so I sat and waited.

"I gotta bad feeling about this. We should just give them a number to call and leave," I told Apple after about thirty minutes had passed.

"Yeah, let's do that."

I was just getting up to the desk officer when a tall dorky-looking detective called me to the back room. He took me into a holding cell.

"Mr. Jones, you're not being put under arrest for anything. This is just until the person you need to talk to gets here. He just called and said that he will be pulling in in just a few," he explained.

I felt a little better knowing that I wasn't being arrested. That told me that they really just wanted to talk to me. But I still didn't understand how they got to Dream. Not long after I was placed in the cell, the detective that came in to talk to me came and got me. He took me to another room that was set up to record him questioning me. Once we were seated he took out his little black book and read me my rights.

"Mr. Jones, do you understand these rights that I just read to you?"

"Yes." Hell, as many times as I'd been read the Miranda rights, I knew them by heart, sadly.

"Do you waive these rights to speak with the police?" he traded his notebook for a yellow legal pad of writing paper.

"Yes."

"Right. Tell me what brought you into the district?"

"I'm here because I heard the police was looking for me. My friend called and told me that the police came to her house looking for me about a shooting."

"Are you talking about the shooting of Deidra Herling?"

"Yeah, I guess that's her name. All I know is people call her Dee."

"How do you know Dee?"

"I don't. I've never met her. All I know about her is what I read on Facebook or seen on the news and that she's my ex-wife's girlfriend."

"What do you mean by your ex-wife's girlfriend? Are you saying she's her friend or that they're romantically involved?"

"They're romantically involved."

"And who's your ex-wife?"

"Donna Jones. But we're still legally married, just separated."

He went on asking me to explain, so I told him about the time I did in the

Feds and how Donna cheated on me both when I was in there and when I got out. I admitted that it hurt, but that I understood it to a certain extent.

"Do it bother you that your wife decided to get involved with a woman?"

"No. I don't care. Things between us is over. I have a girlfriend that I'm good with," I told him, then went on by telling him that I felt kinda responsible for her cheating on me because of all of the bullshit I did in the past. I told him that I was kind of concerned about the controlling way Deidra had over Donna allowing me to see the kids.

"Have you ever met Ms. Herling?"

"No, but I've seen her and Donna together. My stepdaughter told me that they were together. That's how I found out about them."

"How does knowing about the relationship make you feel?"

"It don't make me feel no kinda way. I'm not a jealous or crazy possessive person. I got another woman that I love. I want Donna to be happy, and I guess Deidra makes her that."

"What kind of car do you drive?"

"I got a few cars, but I'm mostly in my full-size Chevy van." At this time another detective walked in the room and asked to see the bottom of my shoes. So that told me that they had footprints, but I wasn't worried because I didn't have on the same shoes. It was a light snow out that night, so, yeah, they should have footprints of the boots I was wearing at the time. I held up my foot so he

could get a look at the bottom of my Air Max.

"I don't think you're being honest with us, Mr. Jones. Can we take a sample of your DNA?"

"Sure." I still wasn't worried because I didn't touch her. I allowed the detective who told me his name was Hooker to swab my mouth. Then he shut off the recorder.

"Jones, we're processing you for breaking the no contact order that you have against you," Hooker told me.

"What? She called me, so I called back because of the kids and what's going on." I dropped my head and let him walk me out of the room.

In the hallway, Hooker handed me off to Mc-Knight, who said he would take me down to processing. The detective led me through the halls in handcuffs that were so tight that I thought my wrist were bleeding.

"Can you loosen these cuffs please? They're too tight."

"You'll be out of them shortly."

I asked him to loosen my handcuffs for the second time because my fingers were getting numb, but he ignored me until we came to a big metal door. McKnight opened the door and then slammed me into it hard, knocking the wind outta me a little. Then he pushed me inside the stairwell and punched me in my body a few times before slamming me back up against the door. He started calling me a liar and telling me that I wasn't going to see my girlfriend or kids ever again. I knew better, but I broke down anyway. I just really wasn't in the mood to keep getting my ass kicked.

I fell to the floor crying like a baby because I knew that I was going to spend the rest of my life in prison for something I didn't set out or try to do. I had an older cousin that told me long ago that killing a kid or a woman was bad luck. Now I see just how true his words are. I stayed on the floor for a few minutes trying to catch my breath.

Chapter 16

Apple's Interview

APPLE WAS NERVOUS AS hell waiting for the detective to come talk to her. When the tall white man walked in, he told her his name then asked Apple her name and address. She watched Detective Hooker write her answers down on a yellow pad of paper. She wanted to ask him what was going on with Ray so bad, but Apple knew he would get into all that soon.

"How long have you known Mr. Jones?"

"A few years."

"How long is a few years?"

"Since about 2009 when we started messing around." She sat up in her seat trying not to look suspect.

"When you say messing around, do you mean you were in a relationship?"

"Yeah, we have an open sexual relationship."

"Okay, when was the last time you saw him prior to today?"

"On the second of this month," she answered, watching him write on his pad and flip between pages. It made her wonder why Ray didn't tell him.

"Tell me about that please?"

"Ray was supposed to spend New Year's Eve with me but stood me up. He didn't call or anything. He just popped up at my house on New Year's Day around 11:00 p.m." She went on to tell him that she was looking out the front window when Ray pulled up in his van. "I was upset with him for standing me up the night before, so I went outside and got in his van to confront him about it away from my kids. I was drunk and high a little from all of the Amsterdam and weed I had been smoking." Hey, you know what they say, "The best lie always got some truth to it," right? "So I got to yelling about where he was the night before, even though I knew he dated other women."

"What did he do when you got in the van yelling

at him?"

"He drove off as soon as I got in yelling at him."

"Did he give you a reason for standing you up?"

"He said he got drunk and lost track of time." Apple told the detective that she had accepted his explanation at first, and then Ray started talking about how his daughter was acting up, and she tried to give him some advice on what to do with her.

"Where was he taking you?"

"Nowhere really. We were just driving around. We went down by Potawatomi Bingo." She told them that she gave Ray some head, and when she was done she got upset again for him standing her up. "I kept asking him who he was with on New Year's because I knew he was with a bitch. I'm sorry, I mean another woman. Then we got into a heated argument and he took me back home."

"What did you do when he took you home?"

"I went in the house and smoked another blunt with my cousin and fell asleep."

Hooker asked Apple when the next time was that she talked to Ray, and she told him tonight, when he came knocking on her door waking her up telling her he needed her to come to the police station with him.

"Did he say why he needed you to come to the police station with him?"

"Yeah, he said the girl who his daughter lives with called him and told him that the police came to her house looking for him. I asked him why they was looking for him, and he said it was for something fucked up." She told the detective that she got dressed and followed him in his van to the district. That's when she saw the other girl, who she figured he spent New Year's with.

"Have you seen Mr. Jones with a gun?"

"Hell, I ain't never seen him do nothing since we been together. Drink, do drugs, or nothing. That's why I didn't buy his story all the way about being drunk that day."

"What was he wearing when he came by your house earlier?"

"What he has on now, I guess."

Detective Hooker asked if he could search Apple's car and home. She told him that she didn't have anything to hide. Then he walked her out to the front desk and told the female officer there to have someone search her car, and if nothing was found, she was free to go. Apple asked him what happened to the other girl she came with, because Ray had told her to take her home in case we got done before he did.

"I'm going to have a talk with her now. You can wait for her if you want. If not, I'll make sure she gets home."

"Okay, I'll wait. I'll take her home," she told him. Then she went and took a seat in front of the window so she could watch them search her car. While waiting for them to finish up, Apple said a prayer for Ray, hoping they would let him go so he could get what he needed to done. She made a plan to go by his uncle's house and tell him what was going on, so he could try to help him.

Chapter 17

Distraught Truth

JUST AS I WAS finishing up my interview of Sparkle Jinxs, I got a call from my partner telling me that Mr. Jones had a change of heart and would like to come clean with us about his parts in the case. I thought it was a little odd that he would change his mind or have a change of heart, as McKnight put it. I'd did my research on Ray Jones, and he was far from new to the system. I really hoped McKnight didn't do anything to fuck up my investigation of this case. I released Ms. Jinxs and then headed back to the south interview room. McKnight was waiting outside the door drinking a coffee when I got there.

"I'm here. What is it he wants to say?"

"I don't know yet," he answered with a devious smirk on his face.

"What's that supposed to mean?"

"I was waiting for you to get here before I went in to speak with him again. All he told me was that he wanted to share something with us regarding the shooting and started crying like a baby," he explained before taking a sip from the hot cup.

"Now why would he want to do that, McKnight? What did you do to him or promise him?" I asked, trying to confirm my suspicion about my gung-ho partner. I knew that he had roughed Mr. Jones up to get him to talk. I just hoped McKnight didn't go overboard with it.

"Hey, let's just say the punk didn't want to finish his walk with me down to processing," McKnight chuckled, taking another drink of coffee.

"I hope you didn't fuck this case up for us!" I snapped, cutting off his laughter.

"Trust me, I didn't. All I did was put a little pressure on him. That's all."

"That's all it better have been." I turned to enter the room. "Turn on the recorder. We need to make sure everything is on point with him from here on out. Got that?" I didn't wait for him to answer. I just walked in the room with Jones.

The first thing I noticed about Ray was he looked like hell. He was very distraught, but other than that, he didn't have any visible bruises.

"You were on your way downstairs, and now you want to come back, why?" I asked as McKnight joined me in the interview room.

"I-I just want y'all to know the truth. I didn't mean to hurt nobody."

"Okay then, tell me what's going on then, Mr. Jones, because I'm here to help you, and I can't do that if I don't know what's going on." I took a seat in the chair across from him hoping that he would look me in the eye when he answered, but he just kept his head down.

"All I want is for Donna to be happy, and Deidra seemed to make her that. Donna told me that she needed time to think about things, and I hoped that we could work things out at some point, but that couldn't happen after our last fallout."

Ray started crying, which made it harder to understand him, because he was already a soft-spoken man. But he told me that he heard from the kids that Deidra was being mean to them and telling them that he was a stupid drunk.

"I know that made you upset." I couldn't understand his response, but he went on talking, telling us that he heard that she was making up stories about him, getting people to try to jump him, and the truth was that Deidra was trying to get him in trouble.

"She had people doing things to me," he said clearly.

I asked him what type of things.

"She had some guys drive a stolen car into the side of my van, and she had someone loosen the lug nuts on my van, and the wheel came off while I was driving with my kids. She told people that we had words and she had to check me. I knew it was her because I seen her with the guys that had been threatening me."

"Okay, Mr. Jones, you got us back here, so tell me how the shooting came about," McKnight demanded.

"I don't know—I don't know how things got to where it was. I don't know how I did it. I just wanted her to leave me alone. I seen her earlier that day talking to the guys in the jeep." He was referencing the group of males that he believed to have been threatening him.

"What happened the night of the shooting?" I asked. Then Jones went on to explain that he had been selling drugs to provide for his family because he couldn't find a job. He told us that on the night of the shooting, he was negotiating a drug deal.

"I noticed that Deidra was following me, so I tried to get away from her, but ended up running back into her on the next block. I kept going at first, but then I got out and went over to her to tell her to leave me alone. When she seen me coming, she pulled over. So I got on the sidewalk so she wouldn't try to run me over. I just wanted her to leave me alone. That's all I wanted to do."

"Did you say anything to her, or did she say something to you?"

"I didn't say nothing but—"

"Did she see you when you walked up to her parked car?" McKnight asked, cutting him off.

"You don't remember, or you know?" McKnight got in his face. "You saw that she was talking on the phone and you snapped!"

"No—no, I didn't know she was on the—"

"You saw her and snapped, didn't you?" McKnight kept yelling in his face trying to get him to admit it on tape.

"No, whoever she was on the phone with is a fuckin liar. She been spreading rumors on Facebook that's just not true."

Jones went on to state that he did not know how many times he pulled the trigger and that he didn't tell anyone else what happened. He also said that he believed that he was defending his life and his family. I knew that what he was saying had to be true because he said things that were not in his best interest to make his point.

"Okay, thank you, Mr. Jones. Is there anyone you want to call?" I was trying to lighten the mood that my partner was making kind of hostile with all his yelling.

"Yeah, I wanna call my daughter and my mother if I can?"

"I don't see anything wrong with that. I'll make sure you get that call as soon as we're done here."

"Hey, since we're giving you something, why don't you tell us where you put the gun?"

Now that was the most helpful question McKnight had asked since I got in here.

"Yeah, we don't want some little kid finding it and getting hurt with it, do we?" I said.

Jones told me that he tossed it in a garbage can

in the alley from his house. "I can't believe I did it. I just wanted her to leave me alone. I'm sorry I took y'all through this!" He shook his head and dried his tears with his hands and then told us that Apple didn't know what she was doing when she made up the alibi for him and asked if we could just let her go because she had kids and truly didn't know that he had killed Ms. Herling.

"Okay, don't worry about her. I just let her go and had someone take Ms. Jinxs home as well."

After I assured him of that, we took him to the place where he said the gun was. It was right where he said it would be. I really didn't believe this was an intentional homicide, and I planned to let my report state as much.

On the way back from picking up the gun, I stopped at Jimmy John's to get something to eat. I asked Jones if he was hungry, because of how long we held him in the interview room. He said yes and that he didn't care what it was as long as it did not have pork or chicken on it. I understood about the pork thing, but I believed Jones was the first black person I'd met that didn't eat chicken.

Once we got him back to the station, we let him eat and then make his phone calls like I'd promised him. I also planned on having a good talk with my partner about the way he handled things with Jones. Had Ray Jones not been so fucked up by the shooting, I believe he would have asked for a lawyer and told him how he had been roughed up by McKnight. And our whole case would've been blown. McKnight should've known by now that I didn't do the good cop, bad cop thing because it didn't work on these guys. As of right now we were lucky, but no one knew what was to come after he talked to his lawyer.

Chapter 18

TIME TO FACE THE MUSIC

ONCE AGAIN I WENT through Booking at the county jail. They retook my photo and rerolled my fingers across a little screen so that it picked up my prints once again for processing. Afterward I found myself a nice spot in the corner of one of the small holding cells. It was cold in the room, as always, but I was alone, which was good cause I didn't feel like dealing with nobody. I lay down on the hard concrete bench thinking of how good it felt to have Deidra's death out. It was crazy because I knew two things at the time. One was that this woman I really didn't know would be forever on my heart, and two was that without a paid lawyer, I may never be a free man again. But I was at peace with it because the truth was out.

I closed my eyes to give them a break. I hoped all of the lies that were being told about me would stop now. The lies about it being a hate crime and shit like that. Yeah, muthafuckas was saying that I killed her because she was gay. They were lying about me being a lovesick husband that killed to get his wife back. That's crazy. Fuck Donna! I wouldn't fuck with her again if she was the

only bitch that could get me outta this hell. I'd rather do the life bid that I was facing than ever fuck with her.

Shit, let me calm down before I give y'all the wrong idea about me. I was missing my loved ones already. The detectives let me use the phone like they promised, so I got to talk to my daughter, my mom, Dream, and Mica. What was beating my mind was the question, "Why were Dream and Mica together?" No, I didn't have anything else to hide from either of them, but I still had mixed feelings about the situation. When I called Pooh's phone, they all were together. There wasn't any hesitation in my heart when I told them all that I loved them. I was thinking Sparkle told Mica that I wasn't getting out, and Mica thought it would be best if my daughter was with her or that it was time for her to meet the woman that held one of the other keys to my heart.

Anyway, I was just glad that my baby was in good hands. I knew her mother was going to try to get her back now that I was in jail, but I still had my rights to my child, and as long as she was still with that no-good punk-ass husband of hers, I'd plan to fight her about my baby.

"Jones? Jones!" called a lazy-looking deputy sticking his big red head in the window of the holding cell.

"Yeah, that's me." I sounded like a broken man even to myself. I got up and walked over to the door, hating to give up my spot in the now funky, crowded cell. I knew I didn't have a choice once my name was called. I took a look over my shoulder and saw that a nasty-looking drunk had taken my place on the bench.

"Come on, you've been fast-tracked up top," the deputy informed me as he locked the cell in the faces of the others behind me who all wanted to know how long they were going to be in the cell. Most of them wanted to get to a working phone. I knew that because I heard a few of them complaining about the one in the cell not working.

"Where did I get fast-tracked to?" I was wondering if the Feds had come to take over the case against me. I had always been told that once you go federal, you stay with the big boys.

"You're going to –." he looked at the card in his hand "– 3B. The faster you get changed, the faster I can get you into a cell with a bed. I got a hot or more like a nice warm meal waiting on you too. I know you didn't want to eat any more of them bullshit sandwiches, did you?"

I shook my head no and followed him into another area of the booking room that held six showers lining the far wall, two concrete benches, and a window with a slot where we stopped so I could pick up my county jail orange monkey suit. "Jones, just get changed. You can shower when you get upstairs."

"Alright." I undressed, tossing all of my personals into a blue laundry bag. Then I dressed in the orange and handed the blue bag back to the inmate behind the window. "I'm ready," I announced to the deputy who was standing in the corner texting back and forth on his phone. "Why am I the only one going upstairs?" I asked while we waited on the elevator.

"I don't know, you must have some kinda pull with

somebody. You're the fastest person I've ever had to take up from booking. Who'd you kill?" he asked jokingly.

"I guess somebody well loved."

The deputy tried to talk to me about my case. He told me that I had been all over the news since the day before. I just listened but didn't answer anymore of his questions. When he continued to press the issue, I told him that I didn't want to talk about it. The doors opened and we got out on the third floor. He took me to the pod that I was assigned to and then placed me in another cell because the cellblock was locked down for the night. I was upset that he had lied to me about me being able to take a shower when I got there. The good thing was that I had the cell to myself. I pulled the flat mattress off the top bunk and added it to the bottom bunk and then made up the bed.

As soon as I got ready to lie down, a chubby, cute light-skin CO came knocking on my door with the warm food that I was promised. She also told me that if I wanted to take a shower real quick I could, but it had to be right then. Hell yeah, I wanted a shower. I set the tray on the concrete slab that served as a table in the cell and rushed out to wash that funky-ass holding cell smell off of me. The five-minute shower felt wonderful after being stressed the fuck out and beat up and then tossed in a dusty holding cell for well over twenty-four hours.

Back in my cell, I sat down on my bunk and forced down the tray of mashed potatoes over cooked corn and something that look like meatloaf. It was a loaf of something, just not really meat. County jail food is horrible. It's known by the inmates and most staff as "slop" or just "chow." Anyway, after I forced it down I got on my bunk and thought about my children. I thought back on the time I took all of the girls roller skating and how much fun we had. My smile quickly turned upside down when Donna's face popped into my head. I thought of all the little moments that I had missed with them because of my marriage to that bitch. I thought of how I would never able to make them up to my babies as I cried myself to sleep. Sleep didn't come to me peacefully. I tossed and turned fading in and out of a dreamlike state until I was fully awakened by the now first-shift officer. He told me that I had court and that they were on their way to pick me up. So I got out of the bed and did my best to pull myself together by brushing my teeth, washing my face, and bowing down to the Lord in prayer. When I walked out of my cell the dayroom was packed with men of all ages, races, and sizes. I noticed many of them whispering about me. I overheard one of them say that I was the nigga who killed that dike bitch over his wife. I just shook my head and kept walking. I got in line with the others that had intake court that afternoon and waited for the two officers to tell us where to go next.

Once I made it down to court staging, I was placed in another holding cell away from the others for some reason. I heard the deputies making jokes about having a star in the mix because of all of the news reporters that were in the court room. I kinda figured they were there waiting to get a shot of me when I walked out there. I wasn't ready to deal with that shit, none of it. I didn't have a lawyer, nor did I meet with a public defender. I didn't know who I was going in the court room to face the judge with that day.

"Jones? Your lawyer's here to see you," a deputy told me, opening the holding cell's door.

"Do you know who it is? I mean is it a PD, or a paid lawyer?"

"I don't know, all I do is movement." The asshole deputy took me to a room, and I sat across from what looked to be the oldest white man in the world.

"Mr. Rayson Jones, my name is John Richards." He didn't bother to stand or offer me his hand or nothing. All that told me that he wasn't on my side. Needless to say, I wasn't looking forward to the court appearance.

I tried to talk to him about what happened in the case and got waved off.

"I haven't had time to go over your case, but I understand that you admitted to killing Ms. Herling, and I don't see any need to have this hearing today. So we are going to waive it and get a date set for trial."

"Do you feel that's the best thing to do? I mean I know I told them I did it, but I didn't mean to hurt or kill nobody."

"That's what trials are for. You can tell your story then. I won't be your lawyer after today, so you can tell whomever you end up with all of that." He stood up and pressed the call button on the side of the door. The deputy came and took me back to the holding cell until it was my turn in court. It's crazy that I never even had a thought of killing that woman but I'm being punished for my care-lessness. I had picked a fine time in my life to try to change. Had I still been on that thug shit, I wouldn't be sitting here now.

Chapter 19

Preliminary Hearing

"THE STATE OF WISCONSIN versus Ray Jones, case number 11-CF-78, first degree intentional homicide," the clerk announced as she opened the proceedings. "Appearances?"

"The State of Wisconsin appears by Bill Markson."

"Good morning. Ray Jones is present and by John Richards."

"Good morning, Mr. Jones. You are here for your preliminary hearing. I have a form signed by you and your attorney, which tells me that the witnesses in this case do not have to testify about what supposedly occurred on January 2. Is that correct?"

"Yes sir," I answered the court commissioner.

"You are thirty-eight years old and you received your GED. Is that right?"

"Yes sir."

"Mr. Richards, your attorney, he read the facts of the case, discussed the evidence with you, and then went over this form with you. Is that true?"

That old muthafucka didn't talk to me about nothing close to that. When I turned to ask him why he didn't talk to me about this shit, the commissioner yelled at me, telling me not to look at the lawyer and to talk to him. I was so pissed.

"Yes," I answered, telling myself that I was going to tell my paid lawyer about all of this shit and let him fix it because it was clear that the fool next to me wasn't trying to help me at all. "The facts of the case involving the death of Deidra Herling, He discussed that with you right?"

"Yes."

"All right. I will accept the waiver. I find it freely, voluntarily, and intelligently made and bind the defendant over for trial."

"Your honor, I am filing a signed and dated information with your clerk, and I am giving Mr. Richards tomorrow if he wants to stop by my office," said the

DA.

"Waive the reading, and we enter a plea of not guilty."

"Why you say I'm not guilty? I told them I did it already."

"Shh, not now. I'll talk to you afterward."

"All right, and I want a copy of the information and discovery," I told Mr. Richards as the clerk read off the next court date.

The deputies came over and walked me out of the court room but not back to the holding cell where I had come from. They had orders to take me right back up to my cell block. They made sure to take me out that way so the reporters could get a few shots of me along the way. I couldn't believe all that was for me. Niggas get killed in the streets almost every day in the Mil, and as soon as I killed a female that thought she was too gangster for TV, the whole fucking city had to stop to watch me.

When I got back on the cell block, the officer informed me that I had a visit. I wondered who it was that had come to see me as I crossed the loud busy dayroom. I walked up the stairs and found the booth that I had been assigned and sat down in front of the monitor as I picked up the phone. After maybe three minutes the monitor came to life, and there was Mica's smiling face. I was shocked. I hadn't expected to see her there or again.

"Hey, mister!"

"Hey, yourself. I'm happy to see you." I forced myself to smile. "I just got back from court a few minutes ago."

"I know. I tried to be there, but I couldn't find the court room. What they say?"

"Nothing. I need a lawyer because the punk that went in with me today don't give a fuck about me. I could've punched his old ass for—never mind. I just need a lawyer."

"Uncle Curt told me to tell you that he's working on that now. He's mad at you."

"I know." I dropped my head because that truth hurt. "Mica, you know I didn't kill her because of what they're saying, right?"

"Look at me."

When I raised my head, she looked me in my eyes so I knew that she was being honest. I saw that she needed me to believe her answer.

"I know you didn't. I'm here because I know you didn't give a fuck about her and because I know that you're mine.

"What else do you know?"

"I know that I love you."

"Love you too," I answered feeling a little better.

"I talked to Pooh."

"Where she at?"

"I think she's at your mother's. All I know is that her mother has been trying to get her. I didn't know if you wanted me to get her or what, so I let Uncle Curt deal with it."

"I thought you took her from Dream or something."

"No, I didn't take her from your other bitch. Rayson, you're lucky I can't get to you or I'd slap that bald-ass head." She threatened smiling.

"No you won't. You might give me some head, but you won't hit me. Then again, you did try to beat me up that one time outside my house."

"No I didn't."

"Yes you did. Remember you thought ol' girl was there to see me?"

"She was there to see you. You know you had plans on fucking that bitch."

"No I didn't. I didn't even know who she was at first. Baby, when I'm with you, you're all I'm with. I don't gotta lie to you about a bitch."

"You better."

"Or what?" I stared into her pretty brown eyes until she smiled "Dream is my friend, that's it, that's all. Yeah, I do love her, but not the way I do you. She gotta girlfriend anyway."

"Ray, that don't mean shit and you know it. You may not love her the way she loves you, but that girl's in love with you."

"No, I think you're misreading things."

"No I'm not. But anyway, I put some money on your books so you can get stuff you need and a phone card to call me."

"You know I don't know your number by heart." She looked at me like I was crazy. "Don't look at me like that. I've never had to dial it, and you just got that number not long ago."

"I suppose you don't know my address either?"

"Nope, I don't." I heard the officer making her rounds and asked her if I could use her pen once she made it to me. I wrote down the info Mica gave me real fast and then resumed my video visit.

"Don't have your ass in there flirting with none of them punk-ass bitches who work here either."

"Baby, stop that. The only thing on my mind is finding out what these folks finna do with me."

We talked a few more minutes, and the screen flashed letting us know that we only had two minutes left to end the visit. Mica promised me that she would be back on my next visiting day before we said our goodbyes. It was then that the tears she had been holding back broke free. The visit ended before I could tell her not to cry for me. In the blank monitor, I saw that I also had tears streaming down my face. I didn't even notice that I had started crying. I cleared my face before I left the booth. On the way to my cell, the officer stopped me to inform me that I was getting a cellmate. Being alone was fun while it lasted.

I put the other mattress back on the top bunk for him and then remade my bed. I stood in the cell's doorway surveying the cellblock to see if there was anyone, I knew and to try and get a feel of who was running what. I wasn't able to see anything that I needed to be concerned about, nor did I see anyone I knew. So I got in bed with a book that I took off the table on my way in from my visit.

I wasn't able to concentrate on reading. My thoughts were racing, my head was hurting, my hands were shaking. Every word that had been said to me in the courtroom, and by Mica that day, was fighting to take over my mind. I was stressed. I put my head under the covers and forced myself to sleep.

Chapter 20

Can't Live with Trash

MY CELLMATE CAME STORMING back into the cell after meeting with his lawyer all worked up.

"Man, these faggot muthafuckas just charged me an' shit!" he told me as he walked the paint off the floor. "Do you know anything about the law?"

I didn't care what he was going through or what they had done to him. I had my own issues to deal with. Hell, I hadn't said another word to him since they had moved him in with me like three days before.

"I know some, but not enough to help you with whatever you're going through. Look, I ain't trying to be no kinda way with you, but I ain't trying to kick it. I got my own shit that I'm trying to process," I told him and then lay back on my bunk and closed my eyes. I wished he had gotten it and shut the fuck up and gone out in the dayroom or something. I was in a better mood because I now had a paid lawyer to help me get the best deal I could outta this mess.

"Yeah, I know. I seen you on the news. That's fucked up how yo bitch did you. I would've killed her ass too."

"Don't believe everything you see on TV. I don't wanna talk about it, really, but that's not how it went down." I sat up in the bunk because he got my attention once he said that he'd seen my case on the news. Hell, I hadn't seen it and really wanted to know what was being said about me.

"Yeah, I hear you. Them white muthafuckas always trying to make something more than what it is." He had started back pacing. "I can't believe these fags charging me with five counts of rape and sexual assault of a child."

I couldn't believe the punk had said what he said.

"What?"

"It wasn't no rape. The lil bitches wanted it. They kept coming to me. Coming over my house asking me to teach them how to be a woman and how to love a man."

"Why would they come to you?" I asked, sitting all the way up now. "What can you teach them about being a woman?" I really wanted to hear what the punk was going to say out of his soup coolers.

"My daughter brought her friends to me so I could show them the way I did her," he explained with not a bit of shame.

"How old is your daughter?" Not that it mattered after he just kinda told me that he was fucking his daughter and her friends. "Thirteen. She finna be fourteen and is already built like her mama." Before I knew it I had jumped up from the bunk, grabbed him by his slimy-ass neck, and slammed him hard into the wall.

"Bitch-ass nigga, I got daughters that age! I should beat the hell outta you for telling me some shit like that!" I snapped, squeezing his throat until his bitch ass started trying to fight for air. "Get your shit and get the fuck outta this cell!" I told him while punching him a few times in the face and gut to let him know that it wasn't a game. Then I pushed him out the door, gathered his things, and tossed them out in the dayroom right behind him.

"Hey! What the fuck is going on?" the officer demanded, running over to where we were, just as dumbass was getting up off the floor.

"I don't fuck with his kind. I don't fuck with baby rapers, so you need to find that piece of shit somewhere else to go because he ain't coming back in here!"

"Jones, step back in your cell and close the door!" he ordered. I did as I was told, and then he asked the punk, "What did he do to you? Did he hurt you in any way?"

The punk looked around the cellblock at all of the other men that were watching what was going on. A few were repeating what they had heard me saying about him.

"No, he just told me to get out. He didn't touch me. I fell." He looked back at me with pleading eyes and said, "I didn't rape nobody, man. I promise you I didn't."

"Fuck you! They kids, bitch-ass nigga. Kill yourself!"

"Everybody, lock in! Lock the fuck in, now!" the officer yelled as he pushed the little red panic button on his radio.

Within moments, the block was filled with officers ready to assist their fellow man. The CO explained what he'd seen and that I told him that Mr. Molester was no longer welcome in my cell. Once the officer was done, his commanding officer walked over to my cell.

"Pop 4!" he yelled to the officer at the control desk. "Mr. Jones, I'm not going to hold this against you. I understand why you don't want to be around somebody like him. But I need to know if I put someone else in with you that it won't be a problem."

"As long as you don't put another muthafucka like dude fool ass in here, I'm good," I answered the Morris Chestnut lookalike. "I got too much going on with myself to be causing trouble for y'all, but I ain't gonna do that." I pointed at the punk. "Not now, not ever."

"Okay, Mr. Jones, I see you've been in this cell with him for a few days now with no issues. What happened today to change that?" he asked, standing in my open cell doorway.

"The only reason we were good was because I didn't talk to him. I didn't know what he was in for until today when he came in telling me about fucking on all them babies like it was okay. I got daughters. I don't wanna hear that shit or be around nobody like that."

"Okay, I'll tell you what. I'm going to move you to 5-D."

"What's 5-D?"

"It's where we house our high-profile inmates."

"Okay, then why don't you move him instead of me?"

"You're high profile, he's not. But he's not going to be placed in GP. I'm putting him in PC for his own protection. If he's dumb enough to go around telling people what he did, then he's a danger to himself. And I don't need that bullshit on my watch."

After about fifteen minutes or so I was taken to the new cell block and placed on a corner cell with a long-haired, light-skin guy. He was sitting on the bottom bunk rebraiding his hair when I walked in. Right away I could tell that he wasn't giving up the bottom bunk, but I asked anyway just in case I was wrong.

"Do you mind if I get the bottom? I take sleeping meds and I don't want to fall off thinking I'm at the bottom."

"No, I got a bad back or something from jumping up and down from there already."

It was bullshit, but I could feel him on all that jumping up and down stuff.

"It's good. I know how to do this." I took the mattress off the top bunk and put it on the floor.

"Man, you don't gotta do that. Just tell 'em to put you in another cell."

"I'm good. I just got moved up here because I put hands on my last baby-raping cellie before I put him out. I ain't trying to be in your business, but why you in here? I'm in for a body, which you might know already from the news. I don't care what you did or didn't do as long as it don't got shit to do with kids."

"Fuck no, I got two bodies. My shit was on TV too. I got a trial in a few days."

"Well, we good then. I'm Ray. Some call me Ace, but it's Assa." I offered him my hand and he shook it.

"They call me Jay. Are you really going to sleep on the floor?"

"Look, I'm from the ghetto, homie. I done slept on the floor before. You just don't forget a nigga down here."

We laughed at the thought and talked some more. Jay was happy to have someone to talk to that'd been to the joint before. This was his first time in and his last time out for a long time if things didn't go right for him—well, life. He asked me if I had seen him on TV or in the papers. I was honest with him and told him that I hadn't seen either since I'd been in this time and that I really didn't watch TV on the streets. I went on to tell him that I wrote books to relax and focus myself.

"I'm looking at life. I know I'ma get it if I can't get a good deal, but if they ain't talking right, I'ma take it all the way and let twelve decide."

"That's what I'm facing too. I shot my baby mama and the nigga she was fucking in my bed while I was at work," he told me. I saw

the sadness in his eyes as he told me what happened. I didn't say a word just, let him talk because he needed to. "I. .. I. .. I just blacked out."

"That's fucked up. She was disrespectful for bringing a nigga in your house like that. Let me guess, on the news they said that I killed ol' girl to get my wife back or some shit, didn't they? But the truth is that I don't give a fuck about my ex-wife and I didn't want to take that woman's life, especially for no shit like that. Man, I shot her because I thought she was reaching for her gun. Hell, I didn't even know she was dead until my best friend told me she saw it on Facebook."

"That sounds like heat of passion to me. That's

what I'm going for, because I just blacked out and pulled the trigger. Heat of passion is for cases like ours. It's when lovers get killed. If I was you I'd ask my lawyer to look into that defense."

"I just got a paid lawyer today, so I'll ask him about it, but I don't think it's the same for me. I'ma sit down and write him tonight right after I finish up this chapter I'm working on."

"What's it called?"

"Facing Life. But it's not about facing time for nothing. It's a story about a nigga that's been through so much shit in his young life that he wants to give up but can't because he's the breadwinner for his whole family. Well, that's how it is in my head right now, but the story will change as I write on."

"Do you mind if I check it out?"

"No, go right ahead. I like the feedback. I just started it, so it's only like sixty pages so far."

"That's a lot. How long is it going to be?"

"I write two hundred-page burners. I try not to write too far over two hundred pages because most people that I know who read urban novels don't really like long stories. They love continuous but not long stories. I try to write for them. But I never know how long a book's gonna be until I'm done."

"How many have you wrote so far?"

"Hell, I don't know. I just write. I started writing back in 2007 just before I got released from the Feds."

I handed him the pages I'd written and then picked up my pen and pad to write my lawyer since Jay was reading what I was working on. My baby mama, Rhonnie, told me that my uncle got him for me after seeing how the one I had wasn't trying to help me. She told me that they were in the court-room both times I went. That made me feel better knowing that they were there even though I didn't see them. It's something about not being alone going through all of this shit that makes it seem easier.

Both Rhonnie and Mica promised that they would be down there to see me every week. They also said that they would be in my corner until the end of time. Though I was feeling good, I also felt dumb for not telling my family what was happening before I turned myself in. No, I didn't regret turning myself in or nothing. I just didn't want them getting in trouble trying to help me. I knew my uncles didn't have any faith in the courts. Hell, none of my family did after all that we'd been through over the years with them.

WIFE 2

Dear Attorney Chaney:

I don't know why I'm writing, to be honest. I was told that you would be taking on my case, so I guess I'm writing to say thank you! I haven't been sleeping much because my dreams are merciless. The knowing that I took a woman's life is pure torture. My mind is everywhere and nowhere at the same time. I am so sorry for the pain I've caused to all the family and friends, hers and mine.

But I just want the truth to come out. I'm not a monster. I did not set out to take her life or even to hurt anybody. I didn't know that it was a phone in her hand.

As I wrote, tears started to fall. I hated to let my cellie see me crying, but when I looked over at him, he was asleep. I guess my book wasn't hitting on shit enough to keep him awake. Either that or Jay was a fast reader. I wiped my face with my hand and finished the letter:

I'm writing to say thank you. It's because of you that my family sees hope even though I know the truth is, there is none.

I ended the letter with that and then took my ass to sleep. Well, I tried to go to sleep, anyway. I think I must have written like twenty pages that night before my eyes gave out on me and I called it a night for real.

Chapter 21

The First Meet with Chaney

"GOOD MORNING, DO YOU mind if we use first names? After all, we are on the same team here, right?"

"I hope we are," I answered so softly it was almost as if I was talking to myself.

I remember how bad my anxiety was in that moment. Only I didn't know that I was deep into one of my spells. All I knew was that I needed to find something to focus on to slow my thoughts enough to help me in the meeting with the chubby, middle-aged, white attorney that my uncle hired for me. Mr. Chaney was smartly dressed and seemed like he was ready for our meeting with my case files and a laptop all set up in front of him.

"It's Ray, right?"

"Yeah, you got it. Most don't get it in the first try."

"I wish I could take credit for knowing it on my own, but I've been corrected so many times by your mother and uncle over the last few days, it's kind of hard to forget." He chuckled. "Well, I'm under the impression that you confessed and that you and your family hired me to get you the best deal I could out of this mess. Am I right?"

"Yeah. Did you get the letter I sent you?"

"Yes, I did."

"So you know how I feel about this, but if the DA ain't talking right, I'm going to take it to trial. The way I see it is life is life, so why not fight?"

"Life is life, you're right about that. I have an offer from the State of thirty-two years to life on the charge of first-degree intentional homicide."

"Fuck that. I didn't intend to kill her or even hurt her!"

"I see that from your statement, but a jury is not going to see it that way. All they're going to see is a big black man that killed a little gay woman that was fucking his wife. If you take this deal, the State says they will let us argue the amount of time in."

"What the fuck do that mean? The time in is life."

"Yeah, life is life, but with this deal it gives you a chance to see your kids and grandkids again before you die. Your mother, uncle, and –" He looked at the file that he was holding "Rhonnie all say for you to take the deal. I think I can talk the judge down to twenty or twenty-five years if you take this."

"I don't know. I ain't feeling the life part, not when I know the judge I got is a hard-ass." I sat back in the chair and thought for a second. "I'll have an answer for you by the next time we go to court. I need to talk to my mother first."

"Okay, that's fine. I'll see you before we go in and see where we are on this deal. So go do what you need to do, and I'll try to see if I can get something solid in writing."

"You do that, and I'll see you then." I stood up and shook his hand before pushing the call button for the officer to come take me back to my cell.

I didn't have long to wait, but it seemed to me like forever in the state of mind I was in. I was trying my best to look as calm as I could on the outside, but in my head the whole conversation was repeating itself over and over. I went straight for the phone once I made it back onto the cellblock and called my mother.

"Hey, Ma! What you doing?"

"Nothing but looking at TV and waiting for Rhonnie to get here so I can be at court for you today. You didn't go yet, did you?"

"No, I just finished talking to the lawyer."

"Yeah, what did he say?"

"He want me to take a deal for life."

"Ray, that's not what he told me when I talked to him. Are you sure you understand him right?"

"Yeah, Ma, thirty-two to life, that's life with the possibility of parole in thirty-two years. That means they will think about letting me go in thirty-two years, not that they will."

"Baby, that's how he explained it to me. Ray, don't fight him. Let him do his job. You wanted us to hire him to get you the best deal he could get you on this mess, and that's what he did for you."

I could hear the pain in her voice as she cried and pleaded with me to take the deal.

"Ma, I'll take the deal, but I'm telling you, it's not what you think. But I'ma take it for you, okay?"

"I just wanna see you before I die."

"I don't wanna talk about nothing like that, Ma.

I'ma do this, but it's not what you think it is." The phone beeped, letting us know that it was time to end the call. "Ma, I'll see you at court. I'm finna call Rhonnie and Mica. I love you!" The call ended before she could respond. I hung up and then quickly dialed Rhonnie's number. She didn't answer, so I called Mica.

"Hey, bae, I was just thinking about you," she answered excitedly.

"Hey, I got court today. They want me to take a deal."

"I know, your mother told me. I can't make it to court today, but I'll be there to see you in the morning, and I want you to call me as soon as you get outta court."

"Okay, but listen. I don't believe y'all know what you're asking me to do with this deal. But I'm not going to go into that with you on the phone right now. I can see that you're cool with it too." I heard the officer calling for everyone to line up by their cells, so I had to end my call. "I gotta go. Tell me you love me."

"I love you and I'm with you until the end."

"Love you too. I'ma call you when I get back from court. Tell

Pooh I said I love her and I'ma call her too. I gotta go now, bye!" I ended the call and then rushed to my cell. As the officer passed, she stopped and informed me that my court date had been postponed until that Friday. I believe that was May 8. I was a little confused and curious about what had happened. I thought maybe Chaney had gotten the deal changed or whatever you wanted to call that offer. Hell, that wasn't a deal in any shape, form, or fashion. I looked around and noticed that my cellie wasn't anywhere to be found. I remember thinking that he might've been on an attorney visit since he had court that following morning. The officer cleared the count, and I went back to the phone.

~ ~ ~

I was alone in my cell with my anxiety way up from stressing over the deal that everybody seemed to think was a good one and that I just wasn't understanding it right. I could feel that the spell that I was having was building to be a bad one. I was having thoughts of building cars and homes. I drew out blueprints for a place I wanted to run to, away from the world, with just my kids, and live. I had to do something to ease my thoughts before I got myself in trouble.

So I started working out in my cell doing pushups while working on the book that I was writing. Every time a scene popped in my head I wrote it down until it was all out, and then I would do pushups until I was happy with the start of the next scene in my head. I was just finishing up a chapter when Jay returned. He walked into the cell looking beat the fuck up.

"What's on your mind, homie?"

"I lost," he said, sounding like he looked.

"You lost what?" I stood up from sitting on my mattress on the floor and leaned back on the desk giving him my full attention.

"I lost the trial. That punk-ass judge wasn't trying to hear shit I had to say!"

"Whoa." I could see that he was serious because he was fighting back tears. "I thought you said you had court in the morning?"

"I just told you that because I didn't want to jinx myself." He sat down on his bunk with his head down. "I didn't trust you. I mean, we're good now, but I didn't know you then."

I could feel where he was coming from because we were in a rats' den. A lot of guys were trying to find out what they could about cases so they could snitch their way home.

"I feel you, my nigg, we good. Now what happened that made the jury decide on your shit so fast?"

"I didn't have a jury trial. It was just me and the judge."

"Why? Was that your doing or your lawyer's?"

"My lawyer's. He thought we would have a better chance with the judge because it was all over the TV and shit."

"Man, it's never a good thing to leave it up to the judge. That's why we been saying we gonna take it to twelve."

"I know, but I already had this set up before I met you."

"So what did the punk find you guilty of?" I asked, sitting down on my bed.

"First-degree intentional."

"Damn. Well, fuck it. Pick your head up, my nigga. You know he finna give you life, but it ain't over for you. You're gonna beat this shit on appeal."

"You really think I got a chance on appeal?"

"With the defense you got, hell yeah! It ain't over, my nigga. You gotta think about your baby because she still needs you," I answered, trying to pull him away from the edge. "I got some news today myself. My lawyer and everybody wants me to take a deal of thirty-two to life."

"You ain't taking that shit, is you?"

"I don't want to, but my mother and everybody wants me to. They don't understand what they asking me to do."

"If you take it you can still get back on appeal, right?"

"Yeah, but it's gonna be hard. But we gotta go hard to get home now. Success is our only muthafuckin' option. Say it with me."

Jay looked up at me looking a lot better than he did when he came back, and smiled.

"Failure's not!" we said in unison.

"I got sentencing next week."

"They just moved my court date back until Friday. I'm hoping my lawyer got the DA to come down on his offer."

The officer released us from our cells for dayroom. I told Jay that I had to go make a call and then went out to call my uncle. I wanted to see if he knew why they moved my court date and to ask him if he thought that was a good deal that, my lawyer came to me with. I knew he knew better than the rest because he'd been through the system many times before in his lifetime.

The whole time that I was on the phone my mind was on my cellie. I hoped that I wouldn't return to the cell and find him hanging from the sprinkler with a bedsheet around his neck.

Chapter 22

Plea Court Day

EARLY FRIDAY MORNING, TWO deputies came and escorted me down to court staging. I was placed in a holding cell with seven others that had court that day. As always, I found an open spot on the bench and sat my black ass in it. I looked around and saw that most of the men in the cell with me were young enough to be in school with my kids. I had to shake off flashbacks of when I was on my way to prison when I was the bright age of six. I wasn't trying to learn what any of them were in for, but I couldn't help overhearing them brag about their crimes like it was a game. It's cool to them right now, but when that judge gave them light years in prison, it wouldn't be then.

I saw how much facing life was killing Jay inside. I tried to help ease his mind by telling him stories of how things were for me the times I went up north to prison. Like so many others, he thought it would be like what he had seen on TV. I taught him a few basic self-defense moves and helped him learn some from a book that he had bought. I was sure that he wouldn't need them because of the way he stayed to himself.

"Jones?" the deputy called me to the door, snapping me out of my head. I gave up my seat on the slab to see what he wanted. "Turn around and put your hands through the trap. You're being moved to your court room." I did as I was told wondering how come my lawyer hadn't come to talk to me. "Chaney's your lawyer, right?"

"Yeah, why?"

"He called and said he would talk to you at court."

"Okay, thanks for telling me because I was wondering where he was."

The deputies walked me down the hall right past Deidra's family members. Some started talking shit and snapping photos of me. I was praying that none of them spit on me. I made it to the holding cell in one piece. After going through that mess in the hallway, I was glad to be in the bullpen by myself. I took the time to get down on my knees and pray for the strength to go on. I made my prayer and then stood, looking out of the window at the traffic below. I saw Rhonnie and her cousin rushing from her white minivan to get to court for me. Seeing them made me smile and feel sadder.

"Ray!" I turned at the sound of my lawyer calling my name and walked over to the bars to talk with him. "Sorry I couldn't get to you sooner. I got another case that's putting me through hell," Chaney said, and then pulled out some papers for me to sign. "How you holding up?'

"To be honest, I'm not feeling this plea, so please tell me that you were able to get it knocked down to anything but this intentional homicide?" I answered, accepting the papers from him so I could read them before I signed my name.

With my thoughts racing the way they were, it was hard to read because I couldn't focus, but I powered through it the best I could.

"I wish I had some good news to tell you, but I don't. This is the deal we talked about. The good thing is this judge we're going in front of today is a lot better than the one we had. I feel he will give us the lowest time we can get because you're taking this plea."

"Now that don't even sound right to you. The lowest part of life is death. Where do I sign so I can get this mess over with? I just want the family to know the truth about what happened instead of the BS the news and papers been putting out there."

"Well you'll get the chance to put it out there today and at sentencing."

"How come I can't get my sentencing today?" I handed him back the papers all signed.

"If that's what you want, then I'll see what I can do. The judge will appreciate the fact that you're not trying to drag this out, so I don't see why he wouldn't honor your request for sentencing."

"The judge is ready to start," the court's bailiff came and informed us.

"Okay, we're ready," my lawyer responded and then turned back to me. "I know you're nervous, but when you get out there, speak loud and clear so the judge can hear you, but don't speak out of turn."

"I'm good. Let's just get this over with."

Chaney reached through the bars and shook my hand before he walked away heading into the courtroom. A short time afterward the bailiff return-ed along with the court deputy to get me and take me into the courtroom. When I walked into the room, I scanned through the crowd that was seated behind a thick glass wall. I saw a few reporters that were seated in the last few rows behind the Herling family. Across from them, I found my family. I saw everyone except for Dream and my dad. But my heart skipped a beat when I laid eyes on my daughter's smiling face. She waved at me just as happy to see me as I was to see her. I was placed at a table next to my lawyer, and then they shackled my foot to the floor under the table. I was told to stand as the judge entered the room.

I remember having a crazy thought of flipping the table and snatching the bailiff's gun, putting it in my mouth, and then pulling the trigger. I was fully aware how close the deputy and bailiff were to me. My thoughts were telling me that it was the end for me anyway with the deal they were offering. The only thing I had to keep me in check was that my daughter and the people who meant the most to me were in the room. Plus, I couldn't let any more of my actions or bad choices conceal who I was. So I started counting backward in my head to try to get past the spell I was having.

"The State of Wisconsin versus Ray Jones, case number 112-GG-007, first-degree intentional homicide with the use of a dangerous weapon. Appearances please," the clerk announced.

"The State of Wisconsin is here by Bill Markson."

"Mr. Jones appears in person with attorney Bob Chaney. Good afternoon, Your Honor!"

"Good afternoon," the judge responded. "You may be seated."

Now that I had something else to focus on, I heard my lawyer thanking the judge for being able to hear my case. The judge didn't look at me like I was trash like the other one did. I noticed that he also made eye contact when my lawyer addressed him, unlike the other judge.

"Thank you for resolving it."

"I also want to thank the court. I know the court has a busy calendar, and this saves everyone a lot of work over the weekend, and also a lot of anxiety knowing there will not be a trial on Monday," Markson said, adjusting his tie. "Judge, the negotiations are these: Mr. Jones has agreed to plead guilty to the charge of first-degree intentional homicide. As the court knows and Mr. Jones knows, that carries a max penalty of life in prison."

When he said that, I looked back at my family to see if they now understood what they had asked me to do. I saw the shocked expression on my auntie's face and a bunch of confused looks on the faces of the others.

"The court has three alternatives: One is to allow Mr. Jones to see a judge in twenty years in order to apply for conditional release. The second is the court could set any time between twenty years and life without any type of supervision. And the third alternative is for the court to sentence Mr. Jones to prison with life without any type of supervision." The DA took a quick pause to look over at me.

I knew he was just trying to see if the information he had given out had shaken me up in any way. It didn't because I already knew what it was, but the gasp that a few of my family members made behind me told us that it had gotten them. Markson grinned and then went on.

"What we recommend is that Mr. Jones, on pleading to the charge of first-degree intentional homicide, will be sentenced to life, but we recommend that after serving thirty-two years in prison he would be eligible to see a court, and at that time the judge will make a determination on whether Mr. Jones is still dangerous or not, to be let back into the community on conditional release, but he will have to serve every day of thirty-two years before he can even apply to see the judge in that type of situation."

"Mr. Chaney, does that correctly state the negotiations?" asked the judge.

"Yes."

"Okay. Is the state going to amend the information to drop 'while armed'?"

"Yes, under the circumstances with Mr. Jones facing life in prison, that seems a rather moot type of enhancer at this point and would move to withdraw that," Chaney answered.

"Okay, Mr. Chaney, can you put the microphone in front of Mr. Jones, please?"

"Yes, but just one other thing before the court begins its colloquy. Attached to the plea questionnaire and addendum, I included the jury instruction 1012 as opposed to 1010. The reason I did that is while the addendum addresses a number of enumerated possible defenses including self-defense, one of the things that the addendum does not address is the question of whether or not there is adequate provocation that would amend by law a jury's verdict, the first degree to second degree."

Chaney looked over and smiled at the DA, who must have forgotten about that little part of the law.

This must've been a part of my lawyer's plan from the start. He could've told me what he planned to do so I could've asked him how he thought it was going to work for getting me less time.

"In my discussions with Mr. Jones, we discussed the provocation defense, and I included those instructions specifically because while there was a history of incidents between these two, Ms. Herling and Mr. Jones, I don't think and believe Mr. Jones agrees with this after we've gone over everything that the provocation situation is going to be applicable because it's not the kind of spontaneous provocation that I think that the statute and the defense require, but it is in some respect an issue that kind of lies there. So I did include that just so the record is complete with regard to that point so that the jury instructions and elements would actually be a three-fold element of intentionality or cause of death by an act and intent at that point. The position that I have taken and Mr. Jones and I take is that it is the intent and then actions that we should reasonably know to cause death with certainty as opposed to the old malice of forethought."

Now I still don't know where he got that I was cool with the intentional part of that, when I had told him from the start that I didn't intend to kill her. But it was said on record, so it would be used on appeal to get me a time cut.

"Let me see if I can just break that down a little bit for Mr. Jones, make sure we are all seeing eye to eye?" the judge said, looking at me. "When you were saying spontaneous, are you talking about adequate provocation that there not be a long delay between the thing that provokes somebody and the actions that they take because if they have a reasonable period of time, they can calm down and they don't. The law doesn't recognize any kind of privilege or expectation the person would act on that motion, is that right?"

"Yes. And also that the instructions very clearly state that you have to be at the point of enraged and so frustrated and so angry that you are in a position where any reasonably prudent person in that situation would be unable to restrain themselves from committing that act. And think under the totality of things. While there was basically some bad blood between the two, it was not a situation that would adequately be covered by those required elements," Chaney butted in and explained like he didn't want me to answer the judge's question a certain way.

"Mr. Jones, do you understand what your lawyer and I are discussing in terms of this possible defense of adequate provocation as a defense?"

I shook my head from right to left but answered, "Yes." I was feeling lied to by everybody in that moment and wondering why they wanted me to spend my life in prison for something I didn't want to do. With my mind racing the way it was, I began to think that maybe I was dreaming, so I dug my fingernails in the back of my hand to be sure I wasn't.

"You're shaking your head no, but your answer was yes. Which one is it?"

"I somewhat understand, but I don't know."

"Let me see if I can break it down a little further, and I invite Mr. Chaney to get involved if you'd like, and then we will start with the basic concept here. The reason we are talking about this right now, Mr. Jones, is that before I can accept your plea, I have to be satisfied that you understand what you're charged with and also that you understand that the State would have to prove that you intended to kill her, which means one of two things. Either that you formed the mental purpose to kill her to make sure she's dead or that you took certain actions that you knew were practically certain to result in death, such as shooting a gun at her. Then there is the third thing the State would have to prove too. If there was evidence that you had been provoked into killing her by some kind of emotional thing, the jury might be entitled to find that you were provoked into this, and therefore that you couldn't be found guilty of first-degree intentional homicide, and the burden would fall on the State to prove that you weren't provoked that way. We have two kinds of cases out there where people have killed when they have been provoked. One of them is a situation, I think, at least suggested by the complaint here, where people have been betrayed in love, so to speak, where somebody has been unfaithful to them. That's the impression I get. It was something Deidra did to you that kind of broke your heart, is that right?"

I said nothing, so Chaney did.

"That's more of a further background. There had been a number of incidents that rightly or wrongly Mr. Jones believes Ms. Herling was behind in terms of intimidation, acts of vandalism to his vehicles, and again a number of these incidents reported to the police hadn't been concretely tied to her, to this. But under all those circumstances, he believed that she was responsible, on the night in question."

"Mr. Jones had some relationship issues, is that right?"

"Right, that's where it first started," the DA answered the judge.

"On the night in question, he saw her car stopped about a block and a half up, got out of his car while armed, walked over to her car to confront her about wanting to be left alone. That alone makes it a difficult situation to invoke either self-defense because he's the one that initiated the face-to-face contact at that point, and the same with provocation," Chaney finished.

"The point I was going to get at, Mr. Jones, is I was keying off of Mr. Chaney about spontaneity, about reaction, this deathly reaction being spontaneous. There have been cases where the law recognizes when somebody walks in on his or her lover in bed with somebody else and pulls out a gun. Maybe in a situation like that, where the person is provoked to such a level of anger or such loss of self-control, we can understand they would do something deadly. But when there is any kind of time between the thing that provokes somebody and the action that they take, the law presumes that during that time a reasonable person can calm down and be affected by their emotions."

Hearing all the talk about the night of the shooting was really fucking with me. That, and with the judge talking so damn slow, wasn't making it any easier for me to keep it together. I began crying. I didn't want them people to see me cry. I knew they would all think I was faking for the court. But I told myself fuck them, and as soon as I got the chance to talk I was going to put the truth out there and take my life back until I could give their's back on appeal.

"And it sounds like in this case, given the intervening business and the fact that whatever she had been doing to you was not immediately before you killed her, the law might make it difficult for you to, I should say make it easy for the State to fulfill that third element. It would be difficult for you to win on the provocation defense. I think that's what we are talking about here and that's what I want to make sure you understand. Do you understand what we discussed, Mr. Jones?"

I didn't know how to respond to it. I made a promise to my mother that I would take this deal for her, and I just wanted to put the mess behind me, so I said fuck it and answered, "Yes."

Chapter 23

The Judge's Conclusion

"**MR. JONES, I WANT** to ask you a few questions to make sure you understand what you are doing here, and then if I am satisfied, then I'll accept your plea. Do you understand that?"

"Yes, sir," I answered, unable to stop my tears from falling or to check my emotions.

"Do you want to pull the mic just a little closer? I want to ask you one more question from the DA here. Is the State going to make a restitution request at sentencing?" the judge asked the DA.

Markson answered yes, so the judge turned to my lawyer and asked if I was going to oppose it?

"Judge, the agreement is that he won't oppose,"

Chaney answered. "Thank you. Mr. Jones, do you understand that the charge against you. .. Well, I should say this, I will acknowledge the State's withdrawal of the allegations in the information that Mr. Jones was using a dangerous weapon, which eliminates the penalty enhancer of five years. So, Mr. Jones, do you understand you're charged with first-degree intentional homicide?"

"Yes."

"Do you understand that if you are convicted of this, the court has to impose a life sentence? Do you understand that?"

Let me tell you that was the hardest thing in the world I tried to do, accepting a life sentence because I made a promise to my mother on something she didn't understand. I wanted so badly to just get up and walk out of there and just let them do whatever it was they were going to do without me there. They could've just come and gotten me when it was over. But my baby was there and I didn't want her to see me run from anything ever.

"Yes," I answered.

"Now, Mr. Markson is right. When we impose a life sentence, there are still three choices for the court to make. I want to make sure you understand those choices. One is the judge will have to say if you go to prison for the rest of your life, but you are allowed to ask to get out at a minimum of twenty years from sentencing. Do you understand that?"

"Yes."

"The other thing I want to make sure of is this. Even though the judge is going to say, well, if the judge doesn't say life in prison and set a minimum eligibility date like twenty years or thirty-two years or forty, whatever the number, that doesn't mean you automatically get out at that point. It just means that's the earliest you can ask to get out. Do you understand?"

"I understand."

"Do you understand that at that hearing the Herling family has the right to oppose your requests? Do you understand that?"

"Yes, sir."

"The other thing that you're going to have to show the court is that you would not be a danger to the community and you have to show that evidence that the court finds clear and convincing. Do you understand?"

Again, I forced myself to answer yes, and the judge went on to tell me that the judge didn't have to grant my release. Once again, my answer was yes.

"Okay, do you understand that the State is going to recommend that you be allowed to get out in thirty-two years?"

"We recommend that he could apply to get out," Markson corrected the judge.

"Thank you for the clarification, Mr. Markson. But, Mr. Jones, do you understand the judge is not required to follow that recommendation at that time?"

"Yes."

"The judge might decide not to give you that right at all and just say life in prison, you never get out. The judge might set your eligibility date sometime after the time asked but before the end of your life. Do you understand?"

"Yes." Tears were really falling from my eyes by now.

"How do you plea to first-degree intentional homicide?"

"Guilty."

"I know you're having a hard time, Mr. Jones. I thought I heard you say guilty, but I want to be sure. What is your plea?"

"Guilty."

"I have a plea questionnaire here. It is signed and dated. Did you sign this?"

"Yes."

"Did your lawyer come over to the jail and talk these over with you before you signed them?"

"Yes."

"Did you see all the rights listed on the document?"

"Yes."

"Do you understand those rights?"

"Yes."

"Do you understand that in particular you're giving up your right to force the State to come to court with a witness and prove beyond a reasonable doubt that you committed the crime?"

"Yes."

"Do you understand they would have to prove that you killed her, that you intended to kill her, and if there is some evidence that you were provoked into killing her that you did not have what we call adequate provocation for killing her? Do you understand?"

"Yes, sir."

"Do you understand that you are giving up that defense? You are giving up the right to say 'I killed her because she provoked me and another reasonable person in my circumstances would have been so bent out of shape that they would have killed her too.' Do you want to give up the right to make that defense?"

"Yes."

"Has anyone made any promises? Wait, I need to ask this: Did your lawyer talk to you about this jury instruction for the State to prove for first-degree intentional homicide?"

"Yes. They gave it to me last night. I sat up all night with it."

"You sat up all night with it. It must have been a difficult night for you. Did you read the whole thing?"

"Yes, more than once."

"Did you understand it?"

"Yes."

"And did you get to ask Mr. Chaney questions about it?"

"Yes."

"I'm sorry, I didn't catch that."

"I – I heard about it from my uncle actually, and I looked it up in the law book, so I talked it over with him."

"And with your lawyer?"

"Yes."

"Did you have any questions for him that he was unable to answer?"

"No."

"Are you satisfied that you understand what the State would have to prove if you took your case to trial?"

"I don't understand the question."

"Okay, before deciding to plead guilty, were you satisfied that you understand what the State would have to prove if you decided to take it to trial? Let me put it this way: You had a choice to make. One choice is to plead guilty, the other choice is to take your case to trial. In making that choice, one thing you have to consider is whether the State can prove its case, right?"

"Yes."

"Okay, has anyone made any promises or threats to you to get you to plead guilty?"

"No."

"I know it sounds like a silly question, you're in jail, but you would be surprised what people say. Did you have any illegal drugs or alcohol?"

"No."

"Do you take any medication?"

"Yes, for depression."

"Did you take the appropriate medication last night or this morning?"

"Yes."

"Is the medication working for you?"

"No."

"How long have you been taking medication?"

"Since 2001."

"So you were first diagnosed in 2001, or is that when you first started taking the medication?"

"When I first started taking it."

"Were you taking meds at the time of the homicide, at the time you killed Ms. Herling?"

"No, not consistently."

"Not consistently. Since you have gotten to jail, have you taken it consistently?"

"They haven't been giving it to me right."

"Tell me more of what you mean by that."

"They gave it to me for like a month and then took me off for some reason. They took it away from me."

"So you were getting it and then they took it away from you about a month ago?"

"A month ago I started taking it again. That's the first time they given it to me since I been here. A week ago they took it away from me, and now they give me a sleep aid or whatever."

"So since that point a week ago, the only thing you've had was something for sleep?"

"Yes."

"Tell me how you feel? As you sit here today in terms of your condition, do you feel like you're kind of riding high? Do you you're riding kind of low? Do you think you're unbalanced?"

"I'm hurting."

"Did you say you're hurting?"

"I just want to give everybody peace."

"Okay, I understand that concern. I need a little bit more information, and I will tell you why I'm asking the question, just so you know. One thing is I have to make sure you understand what you are doing. Some people who suffer from your condition have a hard time thinking through things and understanding and also have a hard time making up their mind. I want to make sure those things aren't preventing you from doing what you want to do here. Let me ask you with regard to your condition, different people experience that differently. Some people are what we call manic; they are always kind of going fast, faster than they can control, and sometimes are so giddy that they can't make decisions for themselves to do anything. They can't feel any of their emotions. They feel like they are very isolated. Would you say that when you suffer from your condition, you feel like what I just described?"

"No. I don't get depressed."

"You don't get depressed a lot?"

"I'm always –" I felt like now them muthafuckas were trying to make me look stupid.

"You're always what, Mr. Jones?"

"Anxious."

"Anxious. Okay, how are you feeling right now?"

"Hurt."

"I'm sorry?"

"All I feel is hurt."

"Can you say more about what you mean by hurt?"

"I just feel hurt. That's it. It ain't nothing else to describe it."

"Okay. So here's the question for me then. Is the hurt you're feeling the kind that makes it hard for you to think through what you are doing here?"

"No."

"So would it be fair for me to say if I had to say it to everybody, that right now you're pretty firm that this is the way you want to decide, the way you want to handle your case. You want to plead guilty instead of having a trial?"

"Yes."

"Okay, I appreciate that. And then two other things I want to quickly double-check. Was there anything that you discussed with your lawyer that you had a hard time understanding that you would like to be clear on before we finalize this?"

"I don't know," I answered, feeling like a tool in front of them. I knew because of the reporters that the whole world could see this.

"You have to speak up just a little bit. I didn't quite hear you, I'm sorry."

"I don't."

"You don't?"

"He doesn't know," Markson butted in, upset

because of how long things were taking.

"I'm not sure I remember what the court's question was," Chaney said, looking up from his notes.

"The question is this, Mr. Jones, and, Mr. Chaney, thanks for making it clear. The question, Mr. Jones, is after you got done talking to Mr. Chaney, was there anything you were unclear about?"

Chaney turned to me and asked me if I had anything I wanted to ask him before we went on.

"No."

"Okay. Mr. Chaney are you satisfied that Mr. Jones understands?" he asked, and then shook his head. "I'm sorry; I keep having questions for Mr. Jones. I'm sorry." He looked back to me. "Do you think you had enough time to talk to Mr. Chaney about your case before you decided to plead guilty?"

"Yes."

"And are you satisfied with the advice you received from him?"

"Yes."

"Okay, thank you." He looked back at my lawyer. "And you are satisfied that Mr. Jones understands all the rights he gives up by pleading guilty?"

"Yes."

"Are you satisfied that he is making the plea freely and intelligently?"

"I am."

"May I accept as true facts stated in the criminal complaint I have here?"

"Yes, and the context of the way we explained it earlier. I believe would be appropriate."

"Okay. Mr. Jones, you had Mr. Chaney describe for me what happened that day when you shot Ms. Herling. Is it true what he told me?"

"I don't remember what you said."

"Okay, well, he talked about how you thought at the time that she had something to do with things happening to your property and she was following you and that you walked back a block to her car and shot her. Is that true?"

"Somewhat."

"I'm sorry?"

"Somewhat."

"Then I have this paper called the criminal complaint. It's the document Mr. Markson issued where he says what he thinks you did. Did you go through this with your lawyer?"

"Yes."

"Is it true what Mr. Markson says in the document?"

"I don't know."

"Mr. Chaney's pulling out a copy of it for you. Why don't we put it in front of you so you can take a look at it."

"Can we ask him what somewhat true means?" the DA asked as I reread the complaint.

"That's what I'm trying to get at, Mr. Markson," the judge told him.

"Judge, my understanding is his point of contention with this

is that, and this goes to the understanding of the two definitions, of intent. When he walked over to Ms. Herling's car, it was not with the intention, again, what we used to call malice of forethought, to kill her. And to the extent that the criminal complaint paints that, that is what he would take exception to. But it was a situation with multiple shots at close range and he acknowledges that there is an element of certainty that someone can be killed if they are shot more than once at close range, which would satisfy the element of intent."

"So I think what you're telling me is that when I read the complaint, I shouldn't read it to say that Mr. Jones intended to kill Ms. Herling when he was walking up to her car, but that at the time he shot her he was practically certain what he was doing was going to kill her?"

"He recognized that it was practically certain that someone would be killed if they were shot multiple times that day," my lawyer explained.

"Mr. Jones, do you understand what Mr. Chaney told me?"

"Yes. Can I say something?"

"Sure."

"I went up to talk to her."

The judge told me to speak up, so I pulled the mic closer.

"When I went up to talk to her, I just wanted to talk to her and tell her to leave me alone because I was not bothering her, I was not doing anything. Forget it, and I don't know, I didn't know, I didn't know how many times I shot. I just reacted, and I didn't know that she died til somebody, my friend, told me and I heard about it on the news."

"You heard what?"

"That she died, and I didn't really, I didn't mean

for it to happen. I just, I just deserve what the court is going to give me."

"I need to make sure we're seeing eye-to-eye here, Mr. Jones. I understand what you're saying, and this is something that happens in these cases, where people do something like this and only realize later just exactly what they've done, but there is an important point for us to make sure we understand before we finalize this. Mr. Chaney told me that as you read this complaint, you agree that if you shoot somebody multiple times at close range like this, there is a pretty high certainty that you're going to kill them and that he says that you were aware at the time you shot her that that's what is practically certain to happen. Do you agree with that?"

"No."

"Okay. Well if you don't agree with that, then we have to have a trial."

"That's fine with me, Judge," Markson said with anger in his voice.

"If I may, Judge?"

"I agree with it. I don't wanna go to trial!" I said, cutting my lawyer off.

"No."

"Hang on for a minute, Mr. Markson." My lawyer looked at me then back to the judge. "Because we've gone over this, and Mr. Jones, you know that shooting somebody, there is a good chance that they are going to be seriously injured or perhaps killed if they are hit by a bullet, correct?"

"Yes."

"And you know if you shoot somebody more than once, the danger of killing them is much greater?"

"I know, yes."

"But you didn't know that you had actually killed her until you heard about it within a day or two, is that correct?"

Again, I answered yes to my lawyer's questions, because I understood everything he was saying, in a way.

"Mr. Markson, does that clarify the record?" asked the judge.

"I don't think an appellate court would think so. I guess what we have to clarify is that he was aware at the time when he was firing the shots into the car that he was practically certain to kill her and that he was aware of that and knew that."

"I think Mr. Markson has a point. The question is this, Mr. Jones," the judge leaned forward in his seat as he spoke, "if you didn't think you would have killed her at the time and only later thought that you did something which would kill her, you're not guilty of this offense. This offense is one that you can be found guilty of only if I am satisfied that at the time you shot Ms. Herling, you were practically certain what you were doing was going to kill her. And so the question is, at the time you shot her, were you aware that shooting her the way you were shooting her was going to kill her and practically certain to kill her?"

The only thing I could do was shake my head no, because I just couldn't do it and it felt good to hear the judge say that I wasn't guilty of that crime. I knew I was guilty of killing Deidra. I just really didn't want to kill her.

"You're shaking your head no. Okay, well, I applaud you for trying to get this resolved, and I think you were trying like you said to put everybody at peace. I appreciate that. I think that's noble, but the thing is, we don't convict people who aren't guilty. We certainly don't convict them of first-degree intentional homicide. I think we need to have a trial, and then we'll think about what the jury thinks about what you were thinking at the time. So I appreciate everybody's effort. I guess we are going to be back over next door on Tuesday, May 23, at 8:30 a.m., for a jury trial."

"Thank you, Judge," Markson said, sounding defeated as he picked up his files.

"Thank you," the judge answered, ending the hearing.

My lawyer told me that he would come see me as soon as he could to talk about trial. Then I allowed the bailiff to take me back to holding until the deputies came to escort me back to the cellblock.

To Be Continued. ..

To order books, please fill out the order form below:
To order films please go to www.good2gofilms.com
Name:_____
Address:_____
City:_____State:_____Zip Code: _____
Phone:_____
Email:_____
Method of Payment: Check   VISA MASTERCARD
Credit Card#:_ _____
Name as it appears on card: _____
Signature: _____

Item Name	Price	Qty	Amount
48 Hours to Die – Silk White	$14.99		
A Hustler's Dream – Ernest Morris	$14.99		
A Hustler's Dream 2 – Ernest Morris	$14.99		
A Thug's Devotion – J. L. Rose and J. M. McMillon	$14.99		
All Eyes on Tommy Gunz – Warren Holloway	$14.99		
Black Reign – Ernest Morris	$14.99		
Bloody Mayhem Down South – Trayvon Jackson	$14.99		
Bloody Mayhem Down South 2 – Trayvon Jackson	$14.99		
Business Is Business – Silk White	$14.99		
Business Is Business 2 – Silk White	$14.99		
Business Is Business 3 – Silk White	$14.99		
Cash In Cash Out – Assa Raymond Baker	$14.99		
Cash In Cash Out 2 – Assa Raymond Baker	$14.99		
Childhood Sweethearts – Jacob Spears	$14.99		
Childhood Sweethearts 2 – Jacob Spears	$14.99		
Childhood Sweethearts 3 – Jacob Spears	$14.99		
Childhood Sweethearts 4 – Jacob Spears	$14.99		
Connected To The Plug – Dwan Marquis Williams	$14.99		
Connected To The Plug 2 – Dwan Marquis Williams	$14.99		
Connected To The Plug 3 – Dwan Williams	$14.99		
Cost of Betrayal – W.C. Holloway	$14.99		
Cost of Betrayal 2 – W.C. Holloway	$14.99		
Deadly Reunion – Ernest Morris	$14.99		
Dream's Life – Assa Raymond Baker	$14.99		
Flipping Numbers – Ernest Morris	$14.99		
Flipping Numbers 2 – Ernest Morris	$14.99		

Forbidden Pleasure – Ernest Morris	$14.99		
He Loves Me, He Loves You Not – Mychea	$14.99		
He Loves Me, He Loves You Not 2 – Mychea	$14.99		
He Loves Me, He Loves You Not 3 – Mychea	$14.99		
He Loves Me, He Loves You Not 4 – Mychea	$14.99		
He Loves Me, He Loves You Not 5 – Mychea	$14.99		
Killing Signs – Ernest Morris	$14.99		
Killing Signs 2 – Ernest Morris	$14.99		
Kings of the Block – Dwan Willams	$14.99		
Kings of the Block 2 – Dwan Willams	$14.99		
Lord of My Land – Jay Morrison	$14.99		
Lost and Turned Out – Ernest Morris	$14.99		
Love & Dedication – W.C. Holloway	$14.99		
Love Hates Violence – De'Wayne Maris	$14.99		
Love Hates Violence 2 – De'Wayne Maris	$14.99		
Love Hates Violence 3 – De'Wayne Maris	$14.99		
Love Hates Violence 4 – De'Wayne Maris	$14.99		
Married To Da Streets – Silk White	$14.99		
M.E.R.C. – Make Every Rep Count Health and Fitness	$14.99		
Mercenary In Love – J.L. Rose & J.L. Turner	$14.99		
Money Make Me Cum – Ernest Morris	$14.99		
My Besties – Asia Hill	$14.99		
My Besties 2 – Asia Hill	$14.99		
My Besties 3 – Asia Hill	$14.99		
My Besties 4 – Asia Hill	$14.99		
My Boyfriend's Wife – Mychea	$14.99		
My Boyfriend's Wife 2 – Mychea	$14.99		
My Brothers Envy – J. L. Rose	$14.99		
My Brothers Envy 2 – J. L. Rose	$14.99		
Naughty Housewives – Ernest Morris	$14.99		
Naughty Housewives 2 – Ernest Morris	$14.99		
Naughty Housewives 3 – Ernest Morris	$14.99		
Naughty Housewives 4 – Ernest Morris	$14.99		
Never Be The Same – Silk White	$14.99		
Scarred Faces – Assa Raymond Baker	$14.99		

Scarred Knuckles – Assa Raymond Baker	$14.99		
Shades of Revenge – Assa Raymond Baker	$14.99		
Slumped – Jason Brent	$14.99		
Someone's Gonna Get It – Mychea	$14.99		
Stranded – Silk White	$14.99		
Supreme & Justice – Ernest Morris	$14.99		
Supreme & Justice 2 – Ernest Morris	$14.99		
Supreme & Justice 3 – Ernest Morris	$14.99		
Tears of a Hustler – Silk White	$14.99		
Tears of a Hustler 2 – Silk White	$14.99		
Tears of a Hustler 3 – Silk White	$14.99		
Tears of a Hustler 4 – Silk White	$14.99		
Tears of a Hustler 5 – Silk White	$14.99		
Tears of a Hustler 6 – Silk White	$14.99		
The Betrayal Within – Ernest Morris	$14.99		
The Last Love Letter – Warren Holloway	$14.99		.
The Last Love Letter 2 – Warren Holloway	$14.99		
The Panty Ripper – Reality Way	$14.99		
The Panty Ripper 3 – Reality Way	$14.99		
The Solution – Jay Morrison	$14.99		
The Teflon Queen – Silk White	$14.99		
The Teflon Queen 2 – Silk White	$14.99		
The Teflon Queen 3 – Silk White	$14.99		
The Teflon Queen 4 – Silk White	$14.99		
The Teflon Queen 5 – Silk White	$14.99		
The Teflon Queen 6 – Silk White	$14.99		
The Vacation – Silk White	$14.99		
Tied To A Boss – J.L. Rose	$14.99		
Tied To A Boss 2 – J.L. Rose	$14.99		
Tied To A Boss 3 – J.L. Rose	$14.99		
Tied To A Boss 4 – J.L. Rose	$14.99		
Tied To A Boss 5 – J.L. Rose	$14.99		
Time Is Money – Silk White	$14.99		
Tomorrow's Not Promised – Robert Torres	$14.99		
Tomorrow's Not Promised 2 – Robert Torres	$14.99		
Two Mask One Heart – Jacob Spears and Trayvon Jackson	$14.99		

Two Mask One Heart 2 – Jacob Spears and Trayvon Jackson	$14.99		
Two Mask One Heart 3 – Jacob Spears and Trayvon Jackson	$14.99		
Wife – Assa Ray Baker & Raneissa Baker	$14.99		
Wife 2 – Assa Ray Baker & Raneissa Baker	$14.99		
Wrong Place Wrong Time – Silk White	$14.99		
Young Goonz – Reality Way	$14.99		
Subtotal:			
Tax:			
Shipping (Free) U.S. Media Mail:			
Total:			

Make Checks Payable To Good2Go Publishing, 7311 W Glass Lane, Laveen, AZ 85339